Witches
Aren't Wicked

The author asserts the right to be identified as the author of this work
which has been asserted in accordance with and under the
Designs and Patents Act 1988.

ISBN: 978-0-9957323-8-8

©SRL Publishing

All rights reserved. No part of this publication may be reproduced,
transmitted, or stored in a retrieval system, in any form or by and
photocopying, or otherwise, without the prior permission of the
publisher.

This book is a work of fiction. Names, characters, places, and incidents
are either a product of the author's imagination or are used fictitiously.
Any resemblance to actual events, places or actual persons, locales is
entirely coincidental.

SRL Publishing Ltd

SRL Publishing Ltd
Office 47396, PO Box 6945
London
W1A 6US

First published worldwide by SRL Publishing in 2021

ISBN: 978-0-99573238-4

1 3 5 7 9 10 8 6 4 2

*To any young girl that has been told you're not enough,
you can do anything you set your mind to*

CHAPTER ONE
Florence

I'm a witch, or so I'm often told, but I'm not dangerous. I'm not *wicked*. I'm just a girl with an ability. An affinity for magic, if you will. The issue is, magic is outlawed for women in the Delgosi Isles, which is where I live. Wizards are common amongst the villages around us, but we must hide. If we don't, we could be imprisoned. We could be *killed*.

My sisters and I slowly found one another, drawn to the missing elements in our own magic. The elements we control are part of us, coursing through our veins like blood. Something that started with just two of us has grown into a coven of six strong witches. We nourished it, made it our own. Our strengths, our weaknesses, our bonds, our powers. Everything between us shaped what is not only a coven but now a family.

'Are you coming, Flo?' I hear from somewhere behind me. I've been so lost in my own thoughts recently that I forgot we were even practising this afternoon. All my concentration is on the trial, the movement. The war. It doesn't matter what you call it, we need to be prepared for *anything*.

I grab my coat and make for the practise space in the woods. The same practise space we've been using since we decided to fight the monarchy. The one right in the middle of Eastfall woods.

Eastfall woods has two main entrances. One to the north and one to the west. We use the entrance on the north side of town, the one used as a shortcut to Midhallow, the next town over, so it's less noticeable than using the entrance on the west. Anyone could be passing through, and we don't want to get caught.

There's a rickety tree about five minutes down the north woodland path, take a left when you get there and continue straight off the road until you reach the viburnum patch. Just beyond that is where you'll usually find us.

When Drusilla and I finally arrive, the four other girls have already started their individual practice. We each have spells that we want to master so we all have the best chance of united success. Me? I'm trying to tune into the spirit sight. I want to be able to see things that people without the gift can't. I want to see the spirits of the dead and the souls of the living. I want to live in both the past and the present. To gain the spirit sight on demand you must be as one with your environment. You have to learn to shut out all external noise and just listen. Listen to the whispers of the gentle wind, the swaying green grass, the emptiness of this dimension and the depth of the next.

I *will* get the hang of the spirit sight. It's just an incantation. Just a couple of words to recite. *Visus spiritus.*

I'm slightly distracted by the sounds of Ottie trying to nail *invisibilia* next to me. *Invisibilia* does what it sounds like, it makes you temporarily invisible.

I'm half inclined to turn around and help but I can't make the spell work for her. We met when she was young and she was already better than any of the wizard's apprentices I knew. Magic is tricky, and unless you have a mentor, it is one of the most difficult skills to learn. Witches don't have mentors. I know she gets embarrassed when she can't pick something up quickly, so I decide to give her a little break.

'Are you okay?' I nudge Ottie's shoulder in a friendly *you can talk to me* kind of way but she doesn't seem impressed.

'I'm fine, it's just taking me longer than I want to get this spell to work.'

'Show me what you're doing, maybe I can help?'

'Like I said before, I'm fine. You have your own spells to learn. It's already November fifth.'

It's been exactly five years since I lost my parents.
Devastation hits me at full force.

'I'm sorry, Flo, I didn't mean to upset you,' Ottie whispers over my shoulder. She lost her parents too, we all have. It's one of the reasons we ended up together.

'It's okay, you didn't mean to. I completely forgot that today was November fifth.' I sigh and turn back to her, 'Do you ever feel like you're forgetting them more each day? Your parents.'

'I've forgotten what my mum looks like... looked like. What she sounded like, what she smelt like. I feel like I've almost lost her completely. Not as much as my Dad though. Addy was always closer to him. I remember when he used to take us out on the water. He loved sailing. We used to pretend that we were pirates looking for treasure. I wish I could remember more detail but every passing year more and more memories fade.' Her breathing gets lighter, almost as if it had lifted a weight of her chest.

'Well then, let's make them proud of you both.'

I hear Addy shuffle over from where she's practising *undas ruinae*, which literally means 'waves of destruction' in Latin. You'll soon learn that Adelaide is our inventor, our atomic bomb. 'I heard you talking about your parents. I'm sorry it's been so long since they were taken from you.'

'Thanks Addy. It means a lot. My mum would

4

have really liked you.' My heart used to shatter into a million pieces when I thought of my parents but now it just breaks a little more each time.

She turns to her older sister, suddenly less mournful. 'I know you can do this. You're just as determined as Mum used to be, maybe even more so. She wouldn't let a couple of bad tries stop her. You just gotta keep going.'

I see a sudden twinkle of understanding in Ottie's bright eyes as she grabs her short hair and ties it up in frustration. Ottilie Lambert has a peculiar look about her. She's petite with deep chestnut hair, which she keeps cropped just below shoulder length, holding the kind of shine that I long for on my blonde hair. She has a face that looks like it has been pinched in at the nose, but her forest green eyes are wide. They look just right against her olive skin

She prepares the spell, commanding the air around her. 'Invisibilia.'

Suddenly, she sparks out of existence.

Then she's back again.

It was less than a second, but it *worked*.

It really worked.

Even if it was just a moment, it's the encouragement Ottie needs to continue.

I know now, with the determination of these girls, we can win this thing.

CHAPTER TWO
June

I'm probably the weakest witch in the coven when it comes to magic because I prefer to use words to fight my corner. It's so simple to manipulate someone with words when you've been doing it your whole life. It may be easier to battle with magic, sure, but it feels so good not to rely on anything but your own brain and body to win. The laws of magic are still so confusing to me, even though I act like I have everything down. *I guess you can just call it witches' intuition.* My entire life I have been told that I'm a natural born leader, and I think all the girls just see me as the person who always has a plan. I mean, I try to always have a plan, my quick thinking helps when we get into sticky situations. The others are keen with their hands, throwing spells and fists around like it's the only thing they know. If anyone caught them doing either, there would be serious repercussions. At least I can't be thrown in jail for calling someone a ninny.

The only spell I really need to know for our plans is *tacit reserare* so it's not something I'm focusing on for now. Whilst the others practise their spells, I start on my speech. *If only I knew how to begin.*

'Dru, how should I address the king when I enter? Your Royal Majesty? Sir? King Ernest? Ernie?'

'How about your Royal Stupidness?'

I can hear the others giggling whilst they're having a break from practice. They're gathered in a circle, drinking the majority of the water in our skins. Training can be hard work, especially when you're not used to practising so frequently and fiercely.

'The task here is to not get executed on the spot, remember?' I say with more force than I mean to, causing them all to turn back to practise. With the rest of the coven preoccupied again with spells and incantations, I find myself a quiet corner and get back to my own work.

I've decided that it's best to write in complete solitude since the others know about four words combined. I say the others, Adelaide is very much the exception. Part of me wishes I could recruit Addy to help with my speech since she is smarter than anyone I've ever met, but she has her own task to focus on.

I pull my knees up to my chest and start reciting out loud what I have so far.

'*From the first ruler of this kingdom until now, women have been shunned and mistreated. We're not allowed to hunt, we're not allowed to fight, we're not allowed to work and most of all, we're not allowed to practise any sort of magic.*'

I spin a web of words through my mind but none of them fit how I want them to. I play the first couple of lines around and around my head, trying to find something to keep the words flowing out of me. Every time I think I've found something that works, I have to scrap it. *Nothing works.* I want to scream but the others will come running to me if I do, and I need the peace to try and focus. I drop my head down to the parchment resting on the tree stump in front of me and cross out the entire beginning of my speech. *Nothing works.*

Clydia creeps over to me. I only know she's there because I feel like someone is watching me. She's very good at that, sneaking up on you and waiting until you jump out of your skin to notice. I think she finds it funny. I turn to face her and notice that my sister looks tired. Heavy black circles lay beneath her piercing blue eyes, a contrast to her warm brown skin. Thinking about it, those dark circles could be bruises. Clydia is always getting into fights. She's got her arms crossed over the long, curly strands of her jet-black hair. She usually ties it into two equal braids down the back of her head but today she's let it hang loose. I like it, she looks much softer than usual. She can be all angles if you catch her in the wrong lighting. I eye my sister up for any more injuries, trying to find tell-tale signs of her being in pain but she shows nothing. I meet her eyes as she opens her mouth to speak.

'I think you should be more aggressive. Say something like *Your hate for women has gone far enough. You make me sick. I have every right to kill you where you sit*,' she says acting calm, like she has no bother if this works out or not, *as usual*.

I roll my eyes and pull myself from the muddy ground. I stumble on my way up but Clydia doesn't move to catch me, she just watches as I steady myself against a tree stump. 'I'll say the same thing to you that I said to Dru. The point of this is *not* to be executed.' *These girls are honestly savage sometimes*.

With my rejection, she disappears back to her spot and begins her incantations again.

I swear, even after so many years of knowing her, I've never heard her move.

I keep going back in my mind to how I met all these girls. How we became this tight knit coven. How we found out we all had magic.

It seems surreal to think that it has been so long yet not long at all and here we are, planning this crazy, dangerous scheme.

Things have been attempted before but nothing

as well planned as this.

We *will* be prepared. We *will* succeed. We *will* be free. *We will*.

CHAPTER THREE
Ottilie

Before

Addy is my younger sister and I've cared for her since our parents died. She was only a kid when it happened, she still is a kid, and she looked up to me. I took us out of town and into Eastfall so we wouldn't be separated. When she screamed, I would calm her, and she always calmed me too. Even after the nightmares, after the anxiety attacks, after the paranoia kicked in. She was there to calm me.

I always thought the fire was suspicious. We would have it lit in the family room all the time, but I know this wasn't the destruction of an ordinary fire. We all know the havoc magic can cause.

Everything has been obliterated, burnt to the ground and nothing left. Don't you see. There has to be foul play involved!

I can't tell you how many times I told Addy those exact words, but she wouldn't listen. Something wasn't getting through. *If there is foul play involved, we have to get out of here before they know we survived,* she would say. *I want to investigate this as much as you do but we don't have time.* She's always been smarter than me. Even back then she knew the right thing to do, it should have been me giving her direction.

It still haunts me that we didn't stay to investigate. We didn't avenge their deaths. We never found out what really happened.

Addy tried to get a job to help feed us, but nobody would take her on. They had their own family to work for them and they couldn't take on the burden of someone else's too. I could see the defeat in her face every time she was turned down.

'No luck again today, Ottie. I just wish someone would give me a chance.'

I couldn't bear to hear those words again.

I took it upon myself to start taking what we needed from those people. I started thieving because nobody would give Addy a job, and it would be even harder for me because as I was older they would have to pay me more. I started out just stealing food from the local market. A loaf of bread here, a couple of apples there, nothing anyone would really notice. I was raised with respect for others, but when you're homeless and genuinely starving you'll do anything for a full stomach.

We had been in Eastfall just over a week and I was scoping out the market for any newcomers when I saw a ship just off the docks. It looked like there had been nobody in it for months, but I'd never seen it before. This was before I knew what a glamour was so it didn't make sense to me yet. It was dirty and it was definitely falling apart but I couldn't take my eyes off of it. There was a handcrafted siren, an evil looking mermaid, on the front of the boat. It was one of the only features not to be drowning in an ocean of green moss.

The siren was calling to me, singing her fatal song.

Before I knew it, I found myself walking towards the docks to explore further.

I kept watch all day to see if anyone came back to the ship, but they didn't. Was it abandoned or was it just temporarily not being used? I didn't really care. I wanted her for my own.

I wanted Addy to come and approve.

I wanted the ship to be our home.

Nightfall came and I knew Addy would be worried if I didn't return soon, so I started to wander back to where we had pitched ourselves. It was nowhere fancy. We had no possessions from home and had barely acquired any since being here. There was an old outhouse on the other side of the town in which we resided. I don't think anyone knew we were there, but we decided it would be best for one of us to be in at all times. Just in case we encountered trouble. We took it in turns to roam the market and I had been out since midday. That was definitely longer than my fair share of time.

You have to move slowly around these small towns, if not people think you've done something that you shouldn't have. I witnessed it on our first day here and I took the unspoken advice on board when starting my own journey. The walk back was only around a mile, but it felt like it was going on forever. The excitement was building up inside me so much I wanted to sprint and scream all the way back, but I decided against it.

Living in an outhouse is as disgusting as it sounds. I found Addy just sitting on the toilet. She wasn't using it, she was just sat there because it was the only place to sit that wasn't the ground. We had a toilet (obviously it didn't flush), a sink (with no running water), and a blanket I had 'borrowed' from a man on the market. One that I definitely planned on giving back. She was twisting her brown hair between her fingers and I could tell my absence had started to worry her.

'Where have you been all this time? I've been worried sick. I thought something had happened to you out there. I thought you had been caugh.t'

'Oka...lisn,...this is gon sond cazy but I've fond a shp we can stay on!'

'You need to slow the heck down because I didn't understand a word of that,' Addy said, looking at me blankly.

I took a minute to collect myself then tried

again. 'This is going to sound crazy but I've found a ship we can stay on! It looks like it's been abandoned at the docks for months, but I've just never noticed it before. Come on, let's go and look.'

She took a moment before she answered, 'Ottie, are you serious? You want us to live on a ship that may or may not be abandoned?'

'Yes,' I thought it was perfectly clear what I wanted. Sometimes Addy is far too protective for her own good. She hates the thought of me potentially getting into trouble. It's almost like she's the older sister.

'Alright, we can look at it in the morning but I'm making no promises to you now. I'm starving, what did you bring back today?'

I realised then that I had forgotten to do the only thing I ever go out for. I forgot to bring us food and water. Suddenly, my mood flattened as my stomach rumbled in protest.

'I'm really sorry, I was so caught up in the idea of us maybe having somewhere to live that I forgot to bring any dinner.' I lowered my head in shame.

I'll never forget the look on Addy's face in that moment. Her bright blue eyes welling up. I could see her trying not to cry. She kept scrunching up her eyes, but a couple of lonely tears slipped out down her cheek. They could have been tears of anger or sadness, or both. It's not like she expected me to bring food back for us, but I'd been doing it for over a week now. I guess we both had gotten used to it.

'Hey, it's cool. We have some bread left from yesterday that I didn't eat. We can share that tonight,' she said, sorrow in her tone. I've never felt more like a failure than I did in that moment.

'The bread is yours. You deserve it.'

'Ottie please, just take some.' She handed me the bread and I tore off a tiny corner. It was getting more stale by the minute. I knew I would want more if I inhaled it like I usually did with food so I nibbled at the edges, trying to make it last.

I didn't realise how tired I was until I laid on the blanket to catch some sleep. It was warm here in the summer, so we slept with the blanket underneath us. We didn't have pillows, so my head was pressed against my left arm where it was bent at the elbow. I've always laid on my side to sleep.

Addy laid down next to me and started tracing circles on my cheek with her thumb. It was something she had done since we were kids. She did it so gently, like she thought I was going to break. I thought I *was* going to break. My stomach growled as I closed my eyes and I felt like everything in me could shatter into a million pieces.

I don't remember falling asleep.

Before I knew it, I heard birds chirping. The sun had risen, and it was time to go back to the docks to persuade Addy to make this ship our new home. The bread from last night was finished so all we had to take with us was the blanket. I shoved it down my trousers which were now far too big and we were on the move.

I was too excited to walk. I just wanted to bound towards the ship and our new future. The short journey felt like it lasted an hour.

We neared the end of the market and it started to come into view. I could see our new home. It did look rather unappealing and I could tell that Addy was disappointed at first glance. She let herself slouch when she was disappointed, and I watched her face drop along with her shoulders.

'We just need to give it a bit of a clean and a lick of paint, it'll be perfect.' I wanted her to love it as much as I did. I think I was expecting too much but it's all I've wanted since we had to leave. A place that we can call ours.

A new home for the Lamberts.

CHAPTER FOUR
Ottilie

Before

I remember feeling like a pirate in search of buried treasure. I wanted us to have everything we needed so I picked my first pocket watch a couple of weeks later. It was solid gold and featured a raven circled with roses on the upper casing. I swung it around and around my fingers in triumph whilst walking back to the ship, back to *our home*. I'm still surprised I was never caught.

We were finally starting to feel more comfortable, so I wanted to be able to *buy* our food rather than steal it. Rich people think they're untouchable. They think I wouldn't dare go near them. How wrong they are. It's so much easier to take from the rich than from the poor. The poor are the people like us who are just trying their best to feed their families.

I had been picking for about three months when I then realised I could get into a tavern unnoticed.

People don't recognise the poor, skinny girl who slides in the door behind them dressed up as a boy. Before the bar staff recognised me, I was already a regular and making money behind the scenes. I had told them my name was Otis.

By making money, I mean playing card games with wealthy men and criminals. They all fancied their chance against a small 'boy'. Playing cards is fairly easy too, especially when every man underestimates you. I had taught myself how to switch cards at the sleight of hand and how to read everyone's poker face. If someone went all in, they probably didn't have anything other than three of a kind, and everyone took an ace as eleven in blackjack. The untouchables are dumb.

I was in the tavern later than I would usually stay that night, on a winning streak with no intention of giving up anytime soon. Someone came over and sat opposite me, they slid a drink across the table and started shuffling the deck of cards. Something felt strange. It wasn't that they hadn't spoken, sometimes people didn't, but it was *something*. I took a sip of the drink and I realised it was a cheap whiskey. I had never really drank alcohol before, but I've been around here enough to know what an expensive drink tastes like, and this isn't one. I could tell I made a face because the stranger looked up from the deck and chuckled. I watched as a crease formed between their eyebrows as they laughed and smoothed itself back out when they stopped.

The stranger had long hair that they kept held in braids. I could tell from just looking at the braids that it was curly, almost like ringlets. They had loose strands that fell round their face so perfectly that it made them look even more mysterious. Their brown eyes looked hungry for triumph. The hood covering their face dropped down behind them and I had to physically stop my jaw from dropping open. I had never seen a woman in here before, let alone one so young.

'Nice deck kid,' she said as she was dealing the cards. This was usually my job, but I was so surprised to see a female in here that I let her get on with it. She looked like she was only a year or two older than me so I didn't appreciate being called a kid by her either.

'Thanks, I stole it from a market a few towns over.'

Lie.

I looked down and I could see that she had dealt the cards for a classic game of Texas Holdem. 'You first' I said, ready to re-establish my control.

'Check. Your turn.'

'Raise you twenty.' I was looking at awful cards, but I could still change that.

'Fold.' *I knew that was coming.*

'Good round. Let's go.'

'You're on, kid.'

We played like that for an hour or so, throwing insults around and playing hands like we had nothing to lose. 'Straight flush, I win,' I said as she looked at me with suspicion in her eyes.

'The name's Clydia. I like you. You're brave.'

'What do you mean?'

'You used magic in a public place to beat me.'

'Keep your voice down. Do you want me to get arrested?'

She let out one of those heavy chuckles again before throwing her hood back up, ready to take on everything that goes bump in the night. 'Come and meet me at sunset tomorrow. There are four of us that practise.'

'Where should I meet you? Can I bring my sister?' *Is she for real or am I being set up?* I thought. But this stranger that I've only known for an hour would have no reason to set me up. Would she?

'There's a rickety tree about five minutes down the north woodland path, take a left when you get there and continue straight off the road until you reach the viburnum patch. Just beyond that is the spot where you'll find us. Only bring women that you trust. The fewer the better.'

With that she left me sitting alone at a table. Curiosity got the better of me and I peeked at her cards.

A royal flush.

A glance back at the table and a quick smile told me she knew I had checked. She raised her hand to her forehead in salute before disappearing through the door.

I pulled my own cloak tighter around me as my next challenger stepped up to the table, followed by the next after I beat him. It all seemed trivial, though, because for the rest of the night all I could think about was the mysterious girl that had offered me a chance.

CHAPTER FIVE
Adelaide

I have always loved inventing things. I remember the first time my Dad sat with me and helped me build a potato clock. He had taught me how do to some really complex maths, too. Maths is the main part of inventing, you see, working out the equations to make everything click as it should, but trust me when I say that science is the fun part.

I suppose we shouldn't really talk about science. It's frowned upon here. Women shouldn't be worrying themselves with things that are *too advanced* for them. I can create things that nobody else has even thought of, but science apparently is *too advanced* for me. Since we're on the subject, though, I have to get this off my chest. I'm about to complete my biggest experiment to date. This is the most advanced physics I have ever taken on. The girls do expect too much of me, but I can't say no. I'll never say no.

Magic kind of defies the laws of science, because according to physics, it shouldn't really exist. There is scientific evidence that can disprove anything if you look hard enough, but how can you disprove something that, to scientists, shouldn't even exist? This will be no common $e=mc^2$. This experiment will be revolutionary. *If* I can just figure it out.

Newton came up with three basic laws of movement. Although they are *called* basic, they're stupidly complicated and it would be too long to go through them now. We just don't have the time. But you should know that I have to use these laws and apply them to something that isn't even considered in the scientific world. I'm going to have to adapt the known rules of how the universe works. Easy, *right?*

I've tried to explain it to Ottie before, but she just doesn't have the concentration. She likes to know things in an instant, but maths and science don't work that way. You have to work for it, be dedicated to the formula. Only then will you get the hang of it. If Ottie can't do it within five minutes she gets bored, and from that boredom, she gets frustrated.

I do worry about her, when she's out there alone. I know I would run into all sorts of trouble being a female scientist if she wasn't there to back me up all the way, but I still worry.

I invented a tracking system a couple of years

ago so I knew where she was if she was out later than I expect, and I still use it to this day. But there's a catch, because there's always a catch. The spell can only track her if she's using her magic. I have a map of the village that I enchanted with my own tracking spell, but rather than having to put a locating spell on her, which she would know about, I've taken it one step further and trapped some of her magic in the map with a binding spell. As soon as she uses magic a little 'X' appears on the map so I know she is safe. She likes to think of herself as a pirate so it's only natural that 'X' marks the spot.

If she knew I had captured and bound some of her magic to this map she would definitely be angry at me, but sometimes you have to upset the person you care about most to make sure they are safe. It's about making the right sacrifices for the right reasons.

'Hey sis, you're meant to be practising. Stop standing around daydreaming.' *It's like she knows I'm thinking about her.*

'I'm actually thinking about our project, thank you very much. It's all well you five coming up with the ideas but I'm the one who has to make the thing happen.' I realise I sound more aggressive than I should have done, but I am under a lot of pressure. I can tell that Ottie didn't take it to heart because she saunters over to me and gives me a wry smile.

'Feeling the pressure a bit are we, Ad? You

25

know I'm here for you to take your crazy behaviours out on, but a little warning would be nice in future.'

'I'm sorry, I've just realised how much pressure is actually riding on me. It's not like I can ask any of you guys to help because I don't even know if *I* can figure out the math.' Something dawns on me as I finish talking. I have five very capable witches around me who all have different strengths. I may have to figure it out, but the others can help once we're on the way to a prototype.

'Clydia, you like to manipulate metals. Do you think you could make a silver sheet so thin it could blow in the wind but with enough structure so it doesn't?' If silver is the best conductor for electricity, then surely it is the same for magic.

'Thin and strong? That sounds like me. I'm sure I can model something after myself.' Everyone is listening in at this point and we all burst into laughter.

I begin brainstorming and it all starts to come together. *A shield*. Months of throwing potential projects back and forth and finally the one that seemed the hardest to achieve is actually something quite plausible.

I watch the others practise for a few minutes, bouncing ideas around in my head as I usually do, before I start my own torture.

Don't get me wrong, magic is in no way torture,

it's one of the best gifts I have ever been given, but it's a lot of hard work. It's a whole load of trial and error, but more than anything, it drains all your energy. At the end of practise I'm just tired and hungry, with a long walk back before I can even sleep or eat.

I didn't realise I had sat down until I had to stand back up and walk back over to the practise area. I close my eyes and focus on the fact that as soon as this is over, I can go back to the ship with Ottie and just crash. My eyes are heavy already and I can feel a dull ache forming behind them. I rub my forehead gently to try and soothe the pain then set off for my spot.

I walk until I can find a suitable target close to where we have been practising. I take a slow deep breath and try to clear my mind. I focus all of my energy on my target, a rather unfortunate rabbit, and whisper the words of destruction. *Undas ruinae.'*

I didn't even hear it hit the ground. I just felt the waves channel out of my hands. The rabbit was alive when I closed my eyes and dead when I opened them. Death has a really strange way of creeping up on you when you least expect it, and even sometimes when you do. It's never going to be easy to deal with, and it's even easier to forget that your life is a gift. You should treasure every single moment your heart is beating in this world.

I stride over to the rabbit and claim my prize. My aim was perfect, but you don't need to have a good aim with *undas ruinae*. You needed control. Magic is all about control. Usually you need a moderate amount of said control along with a good aim and a clear mind, but with *undas ruinae*, you just need a clear mind and a considerably strong level of concentration. I would have zapped the girls where they stood if I weren't paying full attention.

Now I have that sorted, I can go and put this rabbit on a spit and think more about how I'm going to build this thing. *This shield.*

We all pick at small pieces of rabbit around the fire. Everyone is extremely tired but nobody wants to be the first to leave. I'm so comfortable with these girls that the silence of us eating doesn't need to be broken.

As we were finishing up, I watch it dawn upon everyone that we actually have a plan. Nerves start to buzz in the form of jumping knees, twirling hair and paces around the fire. The only person who doesn't seem nervous is Clydia, but then again, when does she?

From now our practise is going to change.

From now, until the end of our days, our practise is going to change. *I'm sure of it.*

CHAPTER SIX
Drusilla

Before

I've always had an issue with needing to be liked. Even when I was a kid, I would charm everyone my parents introduced me to. I was the perfect daughter. My brothers, on the other hand, were *trouble*. My parents shouted at them more times in an hour than they did at me in a whole year. They were always playing pranks on me and I know now that it was their way of showing that they love me. I just wish I knew that at the time. I ended up pushing them away.

When my mother once caught me using magic to heat my bath water, she ran to my father screaming about how I was a spawn of Satan. She told him that I was possessed, and they needed to call the church and ask them to perform an exorcism immediately.

You should know this about my parents, they always loved me, and they would always support me, but they were super religious. So having a daughter that's a witch is probably the single *worst* thing that could have happened to them.

They trapped me in my room after that. Until the priest could get to us and rid me of the demons they thought I had living inside. Essentially, I was stuck because I couldn't have escaped. I knew almost nothing about magic back then. All I could do was play with fire, which was not helpful at all. Fire is unpredictable if you're untrained and although I was angry, I didn't want to set my parents' house on fire.

Father Teddy arrived when I was seriously considering smashing the window and jumping from the second floor of my family home. He was always kind to me, a constant positive presence in my life. He had my back, too. Whether that was making sure I didn't suck my thumb around my parents or tutoring me when I was old enough to learn.

He's the person I need to thank for everything that I have now.

I heard my parents frantically shouting at him all the way down on the ground floor. They must have been really screaming for me to have heard, but I don't remember what they were saying. I just remember giving up trying to listen and moving away from the door, positioning myself in the corner of my room, between my pine bed frame and the far wall. The lilac paint was peeling around the edges and I kept my fingers occupied by playing with a piece until it flaked off into my palm. I didn't want my parents to notice so I stopped picking at pieces of paint and tried to focus on feeling the magic inside me. I still couldn't identify what it felt like, only that I felt ten degrees hotter when flames danced across my fingertips.

Father Teddy asked me nicely to go with him when he finally came into my room. I didn't want to, though, and I made that quite clear by screaming 'NO' at him repeatedly.

Looking back, I can see that it wasn't the best idea, but you have to understand that I was scared. I genuinely thought I was going to die.

I could tell his patience was wearing thin when he looked at me with a mixture of pain and frustration in his usually calming blue eyes. They used to compliment his white blonde hair when he was younger, or so I was told, but now they just seemed to make his sallow skin all the more prominent.

'Drusilla, please. We've known each other your whole life. I want to make this better for you. Trust me, please, just *trust* me.'

I looked at the man who had raised me more than my parents had. *Did I trust him?*

I did.

'Please, don't hurt me,' were the only words I

could manage in that moment.

I walked with him down the stairs and into the reception room without making a single fuss. I still wanted to be the perfect daughter. I wanted my parents to love me more than anything I've ever wanted before, but they wouldn't even look at me when I marched passed them and through the front door. They didn't even let my brothers near me.

I sometimes wonder if they would have changed their minds if they had known this was the last time they were ever going to see me.

Father Teddy and I walked the short journey to the church in complete silence. I was still stunned by my parents initial reaction and I could tell that he had nothing to say to me either. The silence wasn't awkward, though. How could it be when I'd known him my whole life? I'd spent more time with the man next to me now than I had with my own father.

When we started up the front path to the church Father Teddy stopped, but I carried on walking. I wanted to show him that I was stronger than the girl he found almost weeping in her room a few minutes earlier. *I could keep going and just accept my fate.*

'Drusilla, stop. Come back here and listen to me. I'm not going to hurt you.' I turned around, but not because he asked me to. I turned around because I wanted to, because the desperation in his voice tugged at my heart. I walked back towards him slowly and I could see that his slight frame was starting to struggle to maintain balance. That's when I realised how old Father Teddy really was.

'I want you to run from here. There's a boat going from the docks to Eastfall. It's about a day by sea.' He pulled out a black suede bag and held it in front to me. 'Take this and get yourself a ticket. You can stay with somebody I know over there. She used to live here. Her name is Florence Flynn. I helped her get out when her family were taken for harbouring a witch and I want to help you, too.'

Turns out, that very witch was actually our Florence.

I didn't understand what was happening. He was meant to be curing me. 'Father, I…I don't understand.'

Father Teddy took a deep sigh. 'My mother was a witch and she was killed. Her trial was brutal. They thought she was sick, possessed. From that day on, I swore to protect any young witches I could. You're not sick, you have a gift. A gift that Florence will help you learn to control. She's only a couple of years older than you so you should get on better than you ever did with your brothers. It's a small town. Just ask around and I'm sure you'll find her.'

I'm pretty sure my mouth hung open like I was trying to catch flies. 'I can't take this money. You need it.'

'It came from the church's fund that I control. Nobody else needs it. This parish is wealthier than we have ever been.'

I reluctantly picked it from his outstretched hand. The weight of the bag had started to make it shake. I grabbed his arm and pulled him towards me. His footing wasn't great but he managed to stay upright.

I hugged him tight. I felt the tears starting to race out of my eyes as I sniffed and rubbed my face into his chest. 'Thank you, Father. I can never repay you for this. Please promise me that you'll keep yourself safe.'

'I promise.'

'Thank you for believing in me. I love you, and may God bless you from now until forever.'

'I love you too, young Drusilla. Now go, the boat leaves at sunset and we've already started to come into late afternoon. Just stay safe.'

I let go of Father Teddy and ran. I let go of the only person from my old life who believed that I wasn't a monster.

CHAPTER SEVEN
Drusilla

I can see Clydia practising *velocitas* around and around the trees. She keeps doing laps of the base to see how long she can hold the spell, and if she can stop it on demand. It turns out she's good at both of those things. She disappears between a family of leafless trees and appears again moments later, apparently having already circled us twice. I'm getting bored of practising *intus uri* on the barren trees and I want to have some fun. And do you know what *is* fun? Giving Clydia a good scare. I watch the ground for any sign of movement and mutter the spell when she's close enough for the sudden burst of flames to startle her.

It happens so quickly, so suddenly.

She throws out her hands to stop and a flare of pain fills my face as she punches me square in the eye, whilst the momentum of her forces us both to the ground. We land with a thud loud enough to make the other girls stop what they're doing and turn around. Clydia is staring down at me in pure horror. Her current reaction betraying her usual calm and collected expression.

She climbs off of me a lot more gracefully than she fell, and once she's stable on her feet, she holds out a hand for me to grab and pulls me up. 'Why would you do that? I'm going to kill you when you're least expecting it, you moron.'

'I'm sorry, I thought it would be funny.' I replay the moment in my head again before changing my answer. 'Actually, you know what, I'm not sorry. It *was* funny.' I pull my lips together, trying not to howl out in laughter, as she eyes me with genuine fury.

I can tell that she's angry at me but feels somewhat guilty for punching me square in the face by the furrow in between her eyebrows. I reassure her that I'm fine and she's fine but she stalks off and disappears amongst the trees.

Flo rushes over to me to check on my face but I shoo her away, reminding her that it's my own fault.

Before we leave tonight, I want to learn something new. I've pretty much perfected *intus rui* and I know I can be more helpful than just one spell.

Apparently, I'm waiting for my second punch of the evening because I plan to recreate the first, but this time with a twist.

I've heard that you can change your appearance

using a glamour. If I only I can remember the spell.

Think.

Think.

Think.

I close my eyes gently and picture who I want to look like. I place my hands on my cheeks and hope the words come to me. A few moments of nothing pass but as I'm about to give up, my brain has some kind of unbelievable spark. I stand at the outskirts of the clearing and whisper the words that have only just stumbled into my mind; *mutare vultus*.

Nothing feels different. I look down at my hands and they're exactly the same as they were five minutes ago. I let out a sigh of defeat and stroll back to the centre of the practise space, ready to start up my one and only spell again.

I'm bracing myself for the heat that comes along with *intus rui* when Ottie turns around and lets out a very audible gasp. '*Prince Laurence.*' She practically screams in my direction before composing herself.

'Hello. Sorry. Um…Thank you for joining us, your Royal Highness Prince Laurence. H…How can we help you? Did I address you correctly? Oh no, I didn't. Did I?'

I've never seen Ottie so shaken up. If the others weren't staring at me with their mouths swinging open, they would be laughing with the same ferocity as me.

It isn't my laugh that I'm hearing though, it's

deep and full. Full of happiness and ease. I clear my throat and look down at myself again. I am still me, the same Drusilla as when I stepped onto the practise space in the early evening sun. That strong, booming laugh came from within me, though, it came straight from my stomach.

I want to have some more fun with this but the girls will be sick of me by the end of the night, so I decide to remove the glamour. I chant the incantation *vultus mutare* in the voice that isn't my own.

I only know that I'm back to myself when I see the sheer annoyance reflected in everyone's eyes.

Nobody moves.

Until Clydia bursts out laughing.

And it isn't long before the six of us are on the floor along with her.

June wipes her eyes before furrowing her brow. I watch her slow movements with careful eyes. Her own eyes widen before she opens her mouth to speak. 'That's a great idea,' she announces. 'I'd have to figure out the technicalities, but it's a genius idea.'

'Sorry, what is?' I ask.

'Sometimes you lot are so slow,' she rolls her eyes like we're testing her patience one silly comment at a time. 'We glamour ourselves to make the entrance easier. We're a thousand times more likely to get an audience if we're men. It's the way this messed up world works.'

'You want to show *female* competence glamoured as *men*?' Addy asks, considering the proposition carefully.

'Only for entry,' June replies. 'Everything will change when they find out we're women. We need to get our point across as men and then show that we're *actually* women. We show them that they listened to a group of women thinking we were men. It's the best 'I told you' so we can hope for.'

We all agree with June that it would be easier to be get an audience as men, but I can tell that each one of us is sceptical in our own way.

The point of this is to change the way we're looked at, not to be portrayed as deceitful and dangerous.

CHAPTER EIGHT
Clydia

Before

I don't remember having parents. They left me on the street when I was too young to understand. They left me when I was just a kid.

They left me and the institute found me.

I don't remember moving or walking or speaking.

The entire thing feels like a bad dream. It felt like a bad dream at the time, too.

I thought I would wake up in my own bed and my parents would be there, reassuring me of their love.

I wasn't in my own bed, though. I was in the middle of an empty room surrounded by a group of women.

'Where am I? Who are you? Where are my parents?'

A woman with silver hair and a soft gaze was staring down at me, assessing every breath I took.

'You're in our home. You'll be safe here.'

'Please, I want my parents. I want to see them. Where are they?'

'I'm sorry, we don't know. We believe that they left you in the street. They marked you with a hexagram. *They think that you're a witch.*'

'I'm a…*witch*? Why do they think I'm a witch? *Please tell me.*' I'll never forget the look on her face as I pleaded with her for my old life back. If only I knew then that this woman would be my blessing in disguise, my guardian angel.

'I know you have a lot of questions, but we need to get you upstairs. You need to rest somewhere you'll be safe.'

'I don't want to rest, I want to go home.' Tears pricked at the back of my eyes as I hung my head.

'I know, but this is your home now. Come, lift your arms.' I was so exhausted that I did what I was told. The woman, who I now know as Alexina, wrapped my arms around her neck and lifted me. I pushed my head into her chest and fought to keep my eyes open for just a little longer.

The soothing bounce of her steps got the better of me, though, and I fell back to sleep, hypnotised by the swinging of her hips and the rhythm of her breath.

When I finally woke, I was lying on a folded blanket on the floor with some straw underneath for 'comfort'. The light was shining through the window and I could see that there were more sleep stations around me with the same setup. I dragged myself into a sitting position and a different woman raced over to check on me. She introduced herself as Seraphina and told me that she was the home alchemist.

'You're awake, how are you feeling?' She bent down and placed the back of her hand against my forehead.

'I feel tired. How long have I been asleep?'

'It's been two days since we picked you up. From what I could tell you were out there for almost a day before we even found you.'

I didn't even hesitate before I asked about when I could go home.

'I can't answer that right now but how does some healing tea and toasted bread sound?'

My stomach was betraying me, growling for any kind of food. I let out a sigh big enough to cross the entire sleeping quarters and asked my second question of the day. 'Do you have jam here?'

'Strawberry or blackcurrant?' she replied with a small smile. Happy to have diverted away from my previous question.

'Blackcurrant, please.'

'Coming right up!'

I laid in bed another two days after that, drinking different types of healing tea and a mixture of jams on toasted bread. I had just finished a tea that tasted rather like jasmine and one piece of blackcurrant jam on toasted bread when Alexina had walked in.

'Are you ready to come and meet some of the others?' The time I was dreading had arrived. I was scared but I was also bored of being alone. I pulled the blanket off to one side and hauled myself from the floor.

'Do you have any clothes I can wear?' Rather than the cloak and jumper I was sure I had when I arrived, I was dressed in a black cotton robe.

'We all wear these robes so I can't offer you anything more, but there *is* a fresh one hanging near the shower for you.' I hadn't noticed before now but the only two people I had seen were in black cotton robes too.

I tugged at my bottom lip, uncertain of the entire situation, before remembering my manners.

'Thank you.'

The shower room was directly opposite the sleeping quarters and I was more than happy to jump in. I felt so dirty. I had to stretch to reach the button that started the hot water but once it was flowing over me, I started to relax and became much less scared of the day's inevitable events.

'Are you feeling any better?' Alexina was back in the sleeping quarters, waiting for me to return.

'I feel loads better after that shower, thank you.'

'I'm glad. Now let's get acquainted.' Her smile

was as bright as her eyes as she spoke. 'What's your name?'

I was usually so confident introducing myself but I struggled to get my name out this time. 'I'm Cl...Clydia. Who are you?'

'Hi Clydia, I'm Alexina but you can call me Alex.'

'Hi Alex.' A buzzing in my gut told me to ask if she was my friend. She seemed safe. She seemed caring. But then again, so did my parents. I did it anyway. 'Are you my friend?'

Alex let out a gentle chuckle before resetting her features. 'Of course I'm your friend. If you're mine?'

'I would like to be your friend.'

'Then we're friends.'

She took my hand and guided me downstairs to the kitchen. She asked if I wanted anything to eat but I shook my head. I'd eaten enough toast to last me an entire year.

'Where is everyone?' I asked. I didn't expect the kitchen to be empty so close to lunchtime.

'They're in the training room. Let's go and say hi!'

The institute was actually very small. Alex took me down a thin corridor and we reached the end of it in seconds. There was a set of stairs to the left that led down and if you continued walking straight, you would end up going out the front door and back to the streets. We took a left down the stairs and I could already hear more movement.

When we entered the training room, nobody stopped what they were doing. There were roughly twenty girls of all ages throwing punches at bales of hay and hurling knives at sacks of flour.

'Hey girls, this is our new friend Clydia. She's going to start training with us today.'

No response from the masses.

Everyone remained focused on what they were doing.

I'm sure punches were swung harder and knives were flying faster.

I itched to be part of the action, to release some of my anger at my parents, at myself, but there was one small issue. I still didn't know what I was training for.

***

It was over two years before I could go on my first mission. Apparently, there's something questionable about training a six-year-old girl to use a knife as a weapon. By the age of eight I could fight in hand-to-hand combat, I could throw knives with the highest accuracy in the institute, and I could fire every gun I had access to with perfect aim.

In fact, I could do all those things blindfolded.

I still can.

They trained us in ballet too. I hated it but it

was effective.

I can walk into any situation without making a sound and I can balance my bodyweight on any surface.

Alex created an entire training schedule to turn us into animals. Every single thing I did was decided on by her.

She really knew what she was doing.

But I'm sure I would too if I were the one running an illegal hit squad.

CHAPTER NINE
Clydia

Bombing into Dru at twenty miles an hour is probably one of the most embarrassing things to have happened to me in front of the girls. Don't get me wrong, I do feel bad seeing her black eye slowly blossoming, even in the low light of the fire it looks bad, but that's her fault. *She* startled *me*. My only choice here is to get back at her for it.

Whilst the others are pushing through the last part of practise, I'm scheming a prank to play on the queen of pranksters herself. I run ideas through my head with such speed that they can barely form before they're gone again. Until one. One implants in the back of my head, niggling its way back past the others that are still whizzing by.

It's simple yet effective. I just need to get to her room to execute it.

With *velocitas* on my side, I race away from the group as soon as we break practise. My steps are still silent as I make my way through the trees at a speed I haven't reached before, and I am practically invisible as I pass through town. I take back roads and side roads to avoid being caught and only stop to catch my breath when I'm sure no one is around. I give the door handle a little wiggle but Flo never forgets to lock it so I'm forced to do a quick lock pick before barging my way inside. Their home is small and cosy but it doesn't feel cramped. I sidestep passed the creaky floorboard, just because the sound irks me, and take the stairs two at a time.

There's a pitcher of water still sitting next to Dru's bed so I pour myself a glass and relax down onto the cotton sheets covering her straw mattress. I feel like I have all the time in the world so I place the glass on the floor and bring my hands up behind my head, trying to think of a prank that won't upset Florence, too.

I must have drifted off, though I don't remember feeling tired, because I'm jolted awake by the sound of Drusilla's voice filling the empty space downstairs.

I check the door and see that it's still closed. It is. *I'm safe.* I silently pull myself from the bed and pad over to the door. I place my hands against the hard wood and whisper the words *terrorem ianuam.*

Her footsteps are thundering up the stairs as I climb back onto the bed and resume my relaxed position.

48

The thumping of her feet on the stairs has stopped and the clunking of her steps along the landing is growing louder as she reaches me. *One of these days I need to teach her a bit of grace so she doesn't alert every single person of her presence.* She pauses outside her bedroom and clears her throat.

'Clydia, I know you're in there.'

Silence.

'Clydia?' She elongates the end of my name like a question but still I remain quiet. 'You left the door unlocked on your way in.'

The doorknob jiggles as she places her palm against it. I watch the handle turn slowly and my heart skips a beat, preparing itself for the oncoming shock.

The door flies open and…

HHUUUUUUUUUUUUUUUURNK

HHUUUUUUUUUUUUUUUURNK

She leaps back with a high-pitched scream and loses her footing, falling onto her bum. She manages to fling her hands out behind her to avoid smacking her head but she still hits the floor with a loud thud. I want to go and help her but I'm on the floor in fits of laughter. My abs are on fire with the constant tensing and tears are forming in the corners of my eyes as I double over again.

'What on Earth is that?' Flo is running up the stairs at such speed that she could have been running a one hundred metre sprint. She turns to face us and catches sight of Dru on the landing floor, in still shock, and me still curled up on her bedroom floor almost crying with glee. 'Clydia, what is happening? Was this you? *Turn it off!*' She sounds so mad that I instantly snap out of it. Flo is *never* angry so when she speaks in her stern voice, you know you're in trouble. I hop up, my gut aching from the strain of laughing so hard and make my way to the door.

I rest my hands against it and the blaring alarm instantly silences.

'What was that for?' *I really have never seen Flo so irritated.*

'I thought it was funny.'

'Well it wasn't,' she glares at me like an angry parent as she speaks, 'and I think you should apologise to Drusilla.'

'She almost set me on fire a matter of hours ago. I'm not going to apologise!'

Dru finds her feet and offers me a gentle punch on the arm before turning to Florence. 'Flo, chill, it was actually pretty funny.'

She turns back to me and catches my eye, offering a sinister smile. *No hard feelings.* This is Drusilla, though, and I know from the silent confirmation in her deep gaze that I had just declared war.

***

50

Things with Flo are a bit tense after yesterday. I can tell that she's still angry at me for causing Dru to almost fall down the stairs, even though she already got me back fair and square. Nonetheless, I have to take accountability for my actions so I wander over to her and apologise.

'I'm sorry that I took things a step to far yesterday. I didn't think it would affect you both this much.'

She shakes her head before lowering it to her chest. 'I'm the one that should be apologising. I laughed yesterday when you were *'almost blown up'*,' she replies, using air quotation marks. 'I know the mood has been a bit heavy here recently and you were both trying to have some fun.'

'I shouldn't have done it in your home, though. That's your safe place and I should respect that.'

'It was just a bit of fun. All is forgiven, my love.' She pulls me into a quick embrace before holding me at arms length in front of her. 'Now, let's get to practise and show the king what we've got.'

I step back into her arms and squeeze her tight. 'Thank you, Flo.' With that, I turn away and start to practise the two new spells I have planned for today.

I'm hoping that I won't need to use *interficio*, but I should probably learn how to hold the spell properly in case the time ever does come. I shout my absence to the girls.

'I'm going over to that field of rabbit burrows down the path. It's time to practise *interficio* and I would like to keep you guys around for at least the next month.'

Addy turns to me, a look of pure dread in her eyes. '*Please* stay safe. If the spell is too much then don't do it. It is only a backup remember.'

I hear a voice from behind me. *Ottie's voice.* 'If you get the hang of it then you better teach me.'

I don't even get a chance to turn around and respond before Flo spits a quick, 'don't you dare' towards the both of us.

'Okay, okay. I'll be safe and won't endanger any other lives. Damn, Flo, it's like you don't know about my past life.'

I leave with a quick wink to Ottie. A secret promise now bubbling between us.

The field of burrows is only about one hundred paces down the left trail so it doesn't take long to reach my destination. It's the beginning of winter so the fields are empty, but I suspect the burrows are full. In any case, *interficio* won't work if I can't see them. I walk on a little further and stumble across what I can only assume is a farmer's livestock. I debate casting the spell here, but I could be caught. It's also someone's livelihood that I would be taking away. I turn around and walk back to the clearing.

With the girls distracted, now feels like the perfect time to start on my second spell. *Silentium.* I can see June getting frustrated with her speech so a nice break might be helpful for her.

The trick with *silentium* is that it will only work if you are looking directly at your target.

I move slightly so I have a clear view of June. I place my right palm over my mouth and speak the incantation.

The buzzing of her voice in the distance stops.

Good to know it's easy to cast.

June starts to get distressed, but none of the girls are paying attention, too engrossed in their own practise. I keep my eyes planted on her and stride out of the trees until I'm standing in front of her. She looks at me with panic in her eyes, the fear that she had lost the only gift she thought she had. *Speech*. I hold her close, guilt running through me, and say the only thing that will bring the voice back to my friend. '*Dicere*.'

I think she's going to punch me, but I don't flinch back. I deserve whatever karma she wants to send my way. Preparing for the impact of a fist when she raises her arm, I'm surprised when she swings both of them around me. 'You're so annoying but damn you're a good witch. We might actually be able to pull this off.'

'Well I wasn't expecting that kind of response,' I laugh into her shoulder as she holds me tight.

'I'm emotional, okay? How was *interficio* practise? Did it work?'

'So many questions,' I chuckle. 'But no, I couldn't find a big enough group of willing participants.'

'That's a shame. I wish you could have had some practise, but like Addy said, it's just a plan B.' I smile at her and squeeze her back, just like I did with Flo earlier. This behaviour is all very unlike me, but I've been feeling guilty for making fun of June recently. She's been the target of a few of my jokes. I slip from her grasp and step away, ready to continue my original practise.

My role is under control for now so I spend most of the evening helping the others to find their focus. I seem to be mostly Ottie's tonight, though, as I sit and watch her flash in and out of existence for hours on end. She teaches me *invisibilia* too just in case I needed it. It doesn't take me long to get a grip on popping in and out of this dimension, but I can't hold the spell for long, just a few seconds. There was a point earlier this evening when I couldn't see Ottie for almost half an hour. She told me that she was the one tickling my skin when I wasn't paying attention. All so I could watch her pop back in front of me with a smug smile and a sense of achievement.

Half an hour doesn't even compare to a few seconds. Ottilie Lambert has been working hard since the day I met her, and I don't doubt that she was driving herself before that, too. She wants to do something, be someone. We all do.

With another new spell in my grasp, I'm ready to be just as driven Ottie. With her influence, I'm ready to work harder than ever.

CHAPTER TEN
June

There's something I want you to know about my intentions before we go on. I'm not here for me, I'm here for my mother. I don't really want to practise magic, it's brought nothing but destruction to my world since I was a child, but that doesn't mean the people who want to practise it should have to do so in the shadows.

I'm not scared of magic. I'm not scared of being caught using magic. I'm scared of losing somebody else I love as a result of it.

I'm proud to be a woman and my mother was proud to be a woman. She raised me to believe that women may not be seen as equal to men by others, but we are in our hearts, our heads, and our souls. Women are in every way equal to men, other than our genetic make-up, obviously.

She told me I could be anything that I wanted to be. I could be a maid, I could be a healer, I could be a blacksmith, a nanny, or even a farmer, if I wanted to. I just had to say the word and she would be there to support me. She could always lift me up, but I knew that something inside her was sad, even when she was laughing.

My father died from a heart condition just before I was born so it was always just me and her. The two of us against the world.

I knew she could do magic but she never told me. She wanted me to trust her. She was my only source of hope, my only source of comfort, but she kept lying to me. She would wait until I was in bed before she had clients come over. She would heal them or a family member. She would glamour people. All for the sake of a few extra coins in the house. She risked being caught almost every night just to put food on the table.

I hated her for that. *I hated myself for that.*

Almost every day she would have clients. She would never stop but I could tell she was getting tired. All the life seemed to be draining out of her. I stared at her across the dinner table that night and she looked hollow. It was then I knew I had to tell her.

'Mum, I know what you've been doing. I know that food doesn't just appear on the table so why don't you stop lying to me and just be honest. I'm not a kid anymore, you don't need to protect me.' I realise now that I sounded harsher than I had intended to. A look of surprise painted across her gentle face and I felt instantly guilty, but I felt I deserved to know the truth.

Minutes passed and she hadn't said a word. My potatoes were going cold but I wasn't hungry after my outburst. I didn't think I would get a word out of her but as I was about to get up and leave, I heard her say something. It was soft, almost a whisper. I knew she didn't want to say the words out loud but I needed to hear them. I needed the truth from her now more than ever.

'Sorry, I didn't quite catch that.' I wanted her to know that I was serious. I wanted her to know that we were going to have an adult conversation.

'I wanted to tell you.' It was quiet, again, but that time I heard her. Her voice was raspy like she going to cry.

'You wanted to tell me? You've been putting yourself in danger for as long as I can remember. You put *me* in danger.'

'They never would have known you were here. I'm sorry kitten, I should have told you as soon as you were old enough to understand.'

'What do you mean they wouldn't have known? They can see the stairs leading directly up my bedroom.'

I knew I was being mean but I didn't want her to grovel. I wanted her to speak to me like an adult.

'The stairs were glamoured,' the words were

spoken lightly, but I knew the depths of them. *She was almost draining herself to protect me.*

'You're killing yourself, Mum, this needs to stop. I won't let you do this any longer. I'm old enough to work now so I can go out and find a job. There's two of us. You can take a breather.'

She grabbed me by the shoulder and started sobbing. I pulled her in closer and my heart felt lighter having said it all to her. To be honest, my entire body felt lighter. I could have been floating.

We agreed that she would have one last client. They were a regular and she couldn't cancel on them this last minute, or so she tells me. I told her I was going into town and to not worry. I could take care of myself.

I left the house just as the late afternoon breeze was setting in. The summer sun was starting to burn lower as we were heading to the middle of September and I felt good. Mum and I had cried together for ages and everything that was wrong was now right. I kept myself entertained around the market for a few hours, watching buskers and browsing the stalls. The sun had set a while ago and I knew it was time to start heading back. The walk wasn't long, so I was home before the night-time chill set in.

Mum had always left the door unlocked for me when I went out. Lucky for me because today was the one day I forgot to bring the spare key.

The front door was squeaky from years of neglect. We loved our house but any money we had was spent on necessities like food and clothes. I wanted to fix that door one day. When I was earning enough money, I would never have to hear it squeak again.

The squeaky door swung open and I stepped into my home. It smelt like warm bread and vegetable stew. My stomach rumbled. *I really was starving.*

The house was eerily quiet, and my feet seemed to catch every floorboard that dared make a noise. 'Mum?' I called. 'Mum?' I dragged the second call out, a break in my voice towards the end.

No answer.

I decided that she probably had an early night. I ran up to her bed when I heard a scream from out the back.

Mum.

I was down the stairs and through the back door in seconds.

I heard the scream again.

The second one was close, but it wasn't near enough to the house for me to get there fast. I ran in the direction that I thought I heard the noise come from. The screams came again, but this time they were mumbled words. I couldn't quite make them out but the noise confirmed for me that they were straight ahead. Before I could even stop to catch my breath, I saw a dull light shining over the top of an old bush. *I was at the lake.*

'Mum? *Mum!*' I shouted. Desperation filling my heart. I needed her to be here. I needed her to come home with me.

There was no answer.

Instead, a huge man came storming over to me. He was so large that I felt like the ground was going to split underneath my feet with every step he took. When he arrived in front of me, he crouched down like I was a child.

'Your mummy is a witch, darling child, and I bet you are, too. I bet I could throw you in that lake with her and you'd both float. I'd be happy to watch you hang straight after,' his voice wasn't as deep as I had expected.

'My mother is not a witch!'

'Run, June bug, protect yourself from this madness.' It was her voice. She was here and she was alive.

I ran around the side of the bush to find her tied to a chair. Her hands were bound behind her back and her ankles were strapped to the legs. 'Mum. I won't let them do this to you. I won't let them.' I broke down and started sobbing into her lap.

'Move out of the way, kid, or you're going in too!' There was another guy. He wasn't as big as the first one, but he was equally as terrifying.

'I won't let you throw my Mum into the lake.

She's not a witch. I don't know how I can prove it to you but she's not!' I was getting desperate at this point. I could even see her turn away, just so she didn't have to watch her only daughter plead for her life.

'You can prove it to us by letting us throw her in. If she's not a witch, then she'll die with as much honour as you can give a nasty little woman. If she floats, then I'll make sure she *is* put to death.' His wild eyes lit up as he was saying those words to me. All he wanted was to watch women die for crimes they didn't commit.

Obviously, my mum was *a witch, but they didn't need to know that.*

I stood up and faced him. He was much taller than me but, in that moment, I felt bigger than I was. 'Release her.' My voice was monotone, it was firm, I didn't sound like me. Both men stared. I thought I had done it, that they were going to release my mum and we could run away and never look back at this horrible place. How naive I was.

They both laughed at me. It was harsh and heavy. I knew I was going to cry, but I turned to look at my mum and I felt unwavering strength again. I could take on the world. I could end this.

'Silence her,' said the guy I assumed made the decisions, 'and silence the witch, too.'

Before I knew it, I had been knocked to the ground and the other man was on sitting on my back. He had a strip of fabric that looked like it had been ripped from a dirty, old t-shirt. He pulled my head back using my ponytail and shoved the fabric into my mouth. I wanted to spit it out, but it was pushing my teeth together. I wanted to pull away, but he stayed strong on top of me.

He dropped my head back to the ground and pushed it to face my mum. I had a mouthful of grass and dirt in my eyes. The angle my head was at meant I could only just see the legs of the chair my mum was strapped to.

Then I couldn't see the legs.

I thought I had closed my eyes and couldn't open them again.

Stupid.

I could see everything else. A chair doesn't just disappear.

Splash!

The sound crashed through my entire body and drove a pain into the middle of my heart.

I felt like I was drowning on land.

A wave of nothing washed over me, just briefly, before I felt every emotion fully amplified.

I screamed. I kicked. I tried to spin over and throw the man off of me but he wasn't budging. He was just laughing at me. A small girl thrashing at him in the dark.

'Let the witch drown, let the witch burn, let the witch be trapped in an eternity of darkness.' His friend was chanting the words. I thought it was a ritual until he threw his head back laughing, too. Apparently, this was the funniest thing to ever have happened.

The man pinning me down shifted his body weight to double back in laughter. That slight movement meant my arm sprang free so I could push up and whip my body around underneath him. I was halfway to laying on my back before he noticed that I had some freedom of movement, but it was too late for him. I was flat on my back with my fist swinging towards his face.

I had never hit anyone before. This was my fight or flight moment. I swung at his face a second time.

Crack!

He threw himself off of me to cover his nose, blood flowing out both nostrils. It felt good to hit him. I felt a relief. I wanted to go again but I decided against it. I ran. Against all odds, I ran, and I made it home.

CHAPTER ELEVEN
June

I'd been walking for hours and it was nearing the early hours of the morning. The sun would rise before I knew it and I would have to start on my journey again. I was on a quiet path through a wooded area. There didn't seem to be any immediate threat, so I decided to take my chances. I walked about two hundred steps straight off to the left of the path and found a small patch of level ground. I felt safer in these dark woods than I did in the place I used to call home.

I gathered some twigs, sticks and just general dry grass.

I heard a voice in my head. 'Use *parva ignis*,' it whispered. Trying to tempt me to use magic.

I shook my head. Magic had done enough tonight.

I tried to start a fire by rubbing two sticks together. I thought that was what you were meant to do to start a fire, I didn't realise that you needed kindling and everything that goes with it. I was getting colder by the second without the warmth that came with walking. Eventually I gave up, I threw all the sticks I had tried to use in a pile and laid down on my right side. I cuddled my knees to my chest and put my right arm underneath my head.

I don't know how long I laid there, but I knew that I was going to die if I lasted any longer.

I gave in.

I cupped my hands and spoke. *'Parva ignis.'*

A small flame danced over the top of the wood pile. I gently blew on it to encourage the fire to burn brighter and instantly felt warmer.

I laid as close to the fire as I dared and tried to sleep, well rest, for as long as I could. I must have drifted off not too long after because by the time I was aware of my surroundings again the sun was starting to rise.

I sat up slowly, aching all over from sleeping on the hard ground. I fished a chunk of bread from my bag along with some cheese - surprisingly, the cheese kept fresher than the bread in cooler temperatures – and shovelled it down my throat.

I had just finished eating when I felt something hit my face. I looked up and saw grey clouds coming over rapidly. 'Of course it's going to rain,' I sighed. I had been talking to myself a lot since I became a solo girl in the world.

I quickly drank some water out of one of the skins I had brought with me and stood up ready to leave.

After a few quick morning stretches, I started en route back to the path. Counting my steps as I walked.

One. *Two*. Three. *Four*.

By the time I reached the path the rain was really coming down. I didn't realise how heavy it was under the canopy of trees, but as soon as I hit the dirt track, I knew I would be soaked through in minutes if I didn't have shelter. Stopping about two metres away from my original destination, I turned and walked next to the path, but still within the protection of the trees. They had thinned out slightly this close to the track, but they still offered more shelter than what was available a few paces to my right.

The rain started to ease off the closer to midday it got. The sky was still heavy with thick grey clouds, but for now, at least I could start drying off.

It was in the hour before midday and I only had a few miles left until I reached Midhallow. *I could get more food and fill my water skins soon*.

There was one drop. Then another. Then another. Before I could even think about rushing off to the side again, the heavens opened and I was soaked through. There was no gradual beginning to the storm that was coming. It just started and was consistent until it stopped.

As the trees started thinning again, I saw where the woods made way for the road into town. It would have been busy with hunters if it weren't raining so heavily. *'Just a few more minutes,'* I thought to myself. I was almost running by the time I reached the change in the path. I just wanted to keep warm from the ice-cold rain that was hitting me.

When I reached the town there was nobody around. Everyone had herded inside due to the bad weather.

I tried to find some shelter as the first clap of thunder sounded. The thunder was so loud I could feel it vibrating through my entire body. The faster I moved, the faster I would be out of the rain.

It only took me another couple of minutes down the central path to find a weapon maker's shop. They had closed up for the day, but the awning was still out, giving me enough shelter to take cover comfortably.

I settled down on the doorstep and leaned the left side of my head against the red brick wall. This was going to be a longer journey than originally planned, especially if this horrible weather continued. A puddle was beginning to form beneath my feet where the ground sloped downward. I hoisted them up onto the step and turned so my back was resting against the wall. My arms were circling my legs, pulling them closer to me. I rested my head on the tops of my knees and let the past two days come back to me.

As I was drowning in my own thoughts, my breathing started to become unsteady, rapid even. I was straining so hard to get air into my lungs it was almost like I had just run a marathon.

What was happening to me?

I started to shake.

My whole body was moving in time with my rasping breaths.

I started to sob.

The tears were hot against my skin. So hot they burned.

I felt like I was losing control of my body. I kept trying to gather myself but nothing was working.

I couldn't breathe, I couldn't think, and I certainly couldn't speak to the kind person who just happened to be out in this rain long enough to notice me.

'What's going on, love? Are you okay? Do you have anyone I can get to help you?' he asked. His hood was shadowing his face so heavily that all his features were hidden in the depths of the darkness. I only knew he was a man from the tone of his voice. It was deep in places but high in others.

I tried to respond but it came out as a wheeze which only made my breathing worse. I relied on my voice more than anything else and I didn't even have that to guide me through. I felt faint at the thought of it, or maybe I felt faint from the heavy breathing?

'I'm sorry, love, I didn't quite catch that!'

I wanted to scream at him but given the fact I couldn't even form a sentence, I didn't think that screaming would be on the table anytime soon.

'Can't...br...brea...can't breathe' I finally managed.

'Well I can see that. Is there anything I can do to help?' He was being polite, but I knew he wanted to get out of the rain and into the warmth of his home. Probably to be with his family.

I shook my head and tried at what I thought was a smile. He offered a nod in response and left pointing at a brick house just down the road.

He told me that if I felt better any time soon and fancied a hot drink, and maybe some food, then his home was just there. His mum would have some clothes that I could change into so I wasn't soaked through, and his sister had moved out of their home and in with her wife so they had a spare bed I could use for the night.

My mother always told me that strangers do nothing for free. She told me that nobody does. There will always be something they want from you. Whether it is now or in the future. People always come back to call in the favour.

For some reason I trusted this man who had stopped to speak to me in the street. Maybe when I felt more myself, I would go and thank him for his kindness.

After what felt like hours my breathing began to slow. I've never felt like that before. I've never been more scared in my life than when I was sat on that doorstep. I was alone for the first time in my life. *And I mean truly alone.*

My mother was dead.

My mother was gone.

Dead.

Murdered without a trial.

She had no chance to share her story because a man took that away from her.

A man who feared her.

The tears started up again.

I could control this.

***

My feet ached from walking, my head was pounding from the lack of sleep and water, and my face still stung from the night that started all of this. Other than that, the rest of my journey to Eastfall was fairly uneventful.

I finally reached the town at dawn and there were already people creating noise from the market. I guessed they were setting up for the day. I knew I could sweet talk my way into some work if I tried hard enough.

I attempted to brush my fingers though my still damp hair, but it was just knotty. *A ponytail it is then.* I pulled it back and walked confidently towards a kind looking woman selling handmade jewellery, blankets, pillow covers and, strangely, mirrors.

'Hello Ma'am,' I said politely. Making my eyes look innocent but my body grown up. I caught a glance of myself in one of the mirrors she hadn't gotten around to putting on display yet and saw what I looked like for the first time in days.

It could have been worse, but I wouldn't have given me a job.

She jumped and I felt bad for startling her, but I would make her like me soon enough. 'Oh, hello there, honey. How can I help you?' She kept her grey hair tied at the back of her head in a tight bun. You could tell that she had spent her entire life outside in the sunshine from the deep-set wrinkles and sun spots that dotted her skin. For an older woman she looked healthier than me.

'I'm looking for somewhere I can spend my time helping others whilst earning just a little bit of money. My mother died just a couple of days ago and I don't have a father. I've been walking for two days just to get here because I was told I had family in the area, but I don't think that is true anymore.

Please can you help me? Just until I can find a place to stay and a job.' My breathing threatens to betray me again but I manage to keep it under control.

'I'm sorry, Miss, but I have no work for you at the moment. I can barely keep the stall open myself some days. People round these parts buy what they need and not what they want.' She looked as sad as I felt whilst she was letting me down.

'You don't have to pay me for today. I would be happy with shelter and some company. If I do well then we can talk about working for you later, but please just give me this one chance.' I was fiddling with my fingers as I was speaking, letting my nerves show. I glanced over to her and she was staring at me with guilt and hope in her eyes.

'One day. That is all I can offer you,' she said.

'Oh my, thank you.' I knew I had given her the right response when she wrapped her arm around my shoulder and walked with me to the bakery. It was early so the bread was still warm. I could have cried with happiness when I took that first bite.

I spent the entire day chatting to this woman about her life and sold everything I could when the market started to fill up. I could talk my way in and out of any situation I wanted to, so I thought my sale skills were pretty successful.

As we were packing up that evening, she told me that she hadn't *ever* made this many sales in one day. She held out her hand to me and flat against her palm was a delicate silver bracelet. It was connected to a small triquetra in the middle.

'For all of your hard work today,' she winked at me. *Did she know?*

I gently took the bracelet from her hand. 'Can you fix it on for me please?'

She reached for the bracelet and wrapped it around my wrist without a single word.

We smiled at one another again. A big grin that might look strange to others but was only shared between us.

I pulled her in for a hug.

'I'm June,' I said as I left for the evening.

'Cora,' she replied.

'Well it was nice to meet you, Cora.'

As I was walking to find some shelter for the night, a girl caught my arm and pulled me close. She was relatively tall, blonde, and she spoke in hushed tones about the new bracelet now sitting on my wrist.

She gave me an address and told me to swing by this evening if I wasn't busy.

Flo had welcomed me into her home and that's where I stayed until I could afford to find my own place with Clydia.

CHAPTER TWELVE
Drusilla

Last summer solstice was the warmest one we've had in years so Flo thought it would be a good idea to teach us all how to swim. 'We all live by the sea now, *and* it'll be a skill that you need in the future. What if you had to jump off the dock for some reason?'

'Then we could use *levitas*.' I said it as a joke, but sometimes I forget that none of these girls have ever had brothers.

'You can't always rely on magic. If someone saw you that would be the end of you. They would wait until you've climbed out and then throw you back in with your hands bound.'

'Flo, it was a joke. I think learning how to swim is a great idea.'

'I have an idea for something that will make this

easier for us,' said Addy, who was standing in between Ottie and I. We were on board their ship waiting for everyone to join the solstice party the town hosts every year. 'It'll take me about an hour to make one for everyone.'

'Can we help with anything?' Ottie asked.

'No, just keep yourselves entertained and have fun. It *is* the solstice after all.' With that, Addy made for the room that was now her lab and we were left to our own devices on the top deck.

We were just finishing up a game of *'opposites'* - a game in which you have to do the opposite of what the leader says - when we heard Addy climbing the stairs back up to us. She was carrying an armful of grey pieces that she could barely see over the top of. When she reached us, she dumped all but one in the middle of the circle and waited for us to pick them up.

'What on Earth do we do with these, Ad?' asked Ottie, who was now next to me.

'You put them over your head, around your neck like this.' She lifted hers and squeezed it over her ponytail until it was around her neck. *She looked ridiculous.* 'They'll keep your head afloat.'

'How do they work?' asked June.

'That is an awfully long explanation, but just trust me when I say they do,' Addy replied, whilst checking everyone's was secured in place. 'Now we can just jump off the ship and float.'

'Yeah, I don't want to do that.'

'We're not going to do that, Dru.' Flo was laughing under her breath as she spoke.

We could hear the noise from the party and we decided to set off. It was still warm so I hoped the water would be slightly above freezing, too. Clydia was the first one in the sea off the small stretch of sand we call a beach. It was less than one kilometre wide. 'The quicker we get in, the quicker we'll adjust to the temperature.'

'Okay, I'm coming,' I said as I sprinted towards the line where the water met the sand. The sea was strangely soothing against my skin. There were no waves, and I wandered out to where Clydia was waiting for us. 'Guys the water is fine. Come in.'

One by one everyone started to join us. June was the last one in because she wanted to *capture the look of all of our faces, together, in the water,* as she walked to join us. She wants to remember us all together, as one big family.

When we were all in, Flo started to explain the mechanics of your arms and legs when swimming. 'Kick your legs up and down to help with the momentum, whilst pushing your arms forward together, then spreading them apart.'

'I don't understand,' Ottie mumbled to Addy.

Florence must have overheard because not a second after Ottie finished she said, 'I can show you.'

She walked slightly closer to the shore so she could swim back to us. When she was happy that she was far away enough away, she pushed her legs off the ground and started to kick. The way her arms moved was mesmerising to watch. She looked like a real-life mermaid. Almost like she was asking the water to politely move around her so she could fill its original space. When she reached us, she put her feet back to the ground and asked if we had any other questions.

'We can do this one at a time or we can do this all together. It's up to you five, now you know the basics.'

'I think we should all try together. In fact, let's make it a competition. The first to swim ten metres confidently, without cheating, gets to dunk the others underneath the water.'

'Drusilla, that doesn't sound safe.'

I heard Clydia clear her throat as if getting ready to speak.

'I think it sounds great!' June jumped in 'Nothing makes a family like a bit of friendly competition.'

'Okay, then let's do this!' I could tell as Flo said those words, she felt a surge of pride. This was a family. A real family. A dysfunctional, mismatched, unlikely family, but a family, nonetheless.

***

If Addy hadn't invented these weird neck things, I think we all would have been dead. You can't concentrate on magic when every instinct you have is just trying to stay afloat.

We were splashing in the water until dusk, which on summer solstice is very late in the day.

Ottie started it.

She sprayed me so I obviously had to get her back, but she moved. I ended up covering Flo who came over and dunked my head under the surface.

'Hey, I thought you said that was dangerous!' I chided, a mocking tone taking place in my voice.

'Changed my mind, punk.' I saw Clydia creeping, well, creeping as well as she could in the water, up behind Flo. Before I could react, she had pulled herself onto Flo's back and was showering her with water. We were both laughing uncontrollably when Flo managed to buck her off like a donkey ditching its heavy load. She hit the water with a splash before resurfacing seconds later.

'Okay, okay. Back to the life skills,' Flo sung before anyone else could get attacked with a surge of water. We could all swim with the neck float but when we decided to take them off it was a struggle. I was getting impatient when I heard June scream. It was a shrill scream of pain.

'Something hurt me oh my god, something got my leg. Someone help me. It stings so bad!'

Flo rushed over to her since she was the most

confident and we all made for the shore. We *all* managed to swim the ten metres when we trying to get away from whatever had hurt June.

Flo laid her down on the sand when we hit the shore and asked to see where it hurt. She lifted her right leg and showed us the aggressive red string on her calf.

'What is it? Do you know? Please tell me it's not serious.'

'I reckon you'll have to have it amputated.' I feigned panic and horror.

'*No!* I can't lose my leg. Flo, please tell me that I'm not going to lose my leg. I can't do this! Flo, please tell me!'

'Drusilla back off. You can tell she's in pain and this is not the time for your stupid jokes.' She offered me a death stare before turning back to the patient. 'June, it's just a jellyfish sting. You're not going to lose your leg. We just need to get you back to the ship so I can treat it.' Flo then turned to Clydia. 'Can you help me carry her? I don't want to worsen the sting if she has an allergic reaction to it.'

'Yeah, sure.'

'June, listen to me. Clydia and I are going to help you back to the ship. Hold your right leg off the ground and don't put any pressure on it. Can you do that?'

'Yeah, okay, just get the pain to stop!'

We all dressed faster than we ever have before

and set off. It took us triple the amount of time it should have to get back to the ship, but thanks to the lights from the middle of town, where the celebrations were still happening, we could see.

The girls laid June down on the top deck and Flo started dishing out orders. I was tasked with heating some water to clean the sting marks of any dirt. I handed my hot water to Flo with a cloth and she asked for some space. I don't know what happened from there, but June was up and walking within an hour.

She gets so embarrassed when we bring it up, that it comes into conversation more often than you think.

CHAPTER THIRTEEN
June

'June, I just need you to grab a couple of things from the blacksmith and then the prototype will be complete.' Addy looks so proud of herself for doing the impossible. If I'm honest, I'm proud of her too.

'Yeah, that's fine. Just give me a list and I'll head on down.' She hands me a piece of paper with just two things.

'Is this all?'

'Yeah, just those.'

'Okay, no problem. I'll head into town now.'

Today is one of those days that I just want to go and see Cora. I need attention from someone else for a change, and she's the best there is.

I start the quick walk into town with Addy's list in my hand.

I would stop by the blacksmith first and then spend some time with Cora. *I had responsibilities after all.*

The market is busy for late afternoon and I hand the blacksmith the list expecting a wait, but he already had them made up. 'She came to see me yesterday.'

I nod at the scrawny man and take my purse out to pay. 'Paid up yesterday too, Miss. Gave me a bit extra to get them done overnight. Important, are they?'

'Thank you for your quick service sir, but what we are doing is top secret.'

He raises his eyebrow at me in surprise. 'Right, oh.'

I pick the bag off the wooden workbench he's using as a front desk and call out my thanks again before disappearing into the street.

The blacksmith is fairly close to the bakery. It's also close enough to Cora that I can grab her a hot drink and a pastry and it still be hot when I reach her. She can always sense me coming so when I cross into the back of the stall, she doesn't even turn to greet me.

'A hot tea and a game pastry.' I pass the food warming my hands over to her with a soft smile.

'You've always known how to treat me,' she replies, taking them with more grace than I ever could. We sit in silence whilst she eats, her blue eyes peering back at me gratefully every time she takes a sip of tea.

'What's on your mind, dear?' she asks, brushing

the pastry flakes that had escaped onto her clothes.

'We're leaving tomorrow, I think.'

'That's come around quickly. Are you ready for it?'

'Everything ran smoothly the last time we tried.' I twist my bracelet around and around my wrist.

'I made more of those, you know, but I could never bring myself to sell them.'

'Why not?'

'Because you deserve to have the only one.' My heart starts to melt. This woman is alone outside of this market. She has no family, only the friends from the stalls around her. She deserves more than I do.

'Thank you,' I reply. 'How many more did you make?'

'Five. I made six in total. Seems almost perfect, doesn't it? Like destiny. You should take them. I'll never sell them, and it beats them sitting around getting dusty.'

'How much?'

'A tea and a pastry.' She winks at me before offering a flippant smile. 'Oh, and it looks like you've paid up front.'

'I can't just take these from you.'

'Then think of them as a gift for you all. Goodness knows you need something for yourselves at the moment.'

I don't deserve her kindness. 'Thank you, Cora.'

I gather up my things and give her a quick kiss

on the cheek. Leaving with the promise of a proper meal together when I return.

When I reached the viburnum patch, I can hear the girls shouting at each other. 'What on Earth are they doing now?' I murmur under my breath.

The girls aren't shouting at each other in anger but humouring one other. Throwing insults around like their mouths are already contaminated with them.

'I'm back,' I chime. Addy reaches over for the bag and I stop her. 'Can you all come here for a minute?' I'm greeted with puzzled looks, but we all gathered in a small corner.

'So, the likelihood is that our journey begins tomorrow. It's going to be long, it's going to be dangerous and it's going to test our strength throughout. I got us something to remind us that in unity there is strength. As long as we have each other, we have everything that we will ever need. The rest is just extra. We are strong. We are brave. We are sisters. We are *women*.' I pick the bracelets from the bag one by one. Cora had packaged them nicely before I left and I didn't want to mess them up.

'What are these?' asks Ottie when everyone is holding a box.

'Open them.' There's a minute of rustling paper before everyone has theirs out. They all look at me and then back to the bracelets, as if they can't believe they're holding something so beautiful.

'It's the triquetra,' I explain. 'It symbolises the three faces of a goddess. Balance of the Mind, Body and Spirit. You're all goddesses to me. Thank you for fighting alongside me.'

Nobody says anything.

'Oh, you all hate them don't you.'

Clydia looks up at me then, with tears in her eyes. I've never seen her cry other than in laughter.

'You always know the right things to say, don't you?' She envelopes me in a hug and asks me to put her bracelet on.

Everyone else seems to realise that they should speak too. So after a chorus of thanks, mixed with sobs, and the dainty tinkling of metal as bracelets are fastened, we all embrace one another.

In this moment, it's just us. Our coven. Our family.

CHAPTER FOURTEEN
Clydia

Before

I haven't told the girls yet but I've met Prince Aeron in the past. I was hired to do a job to silently remove someone important in his life. He was never meant to know that it happened but unfortunately he did.

He was there when he shouldn't have been.

I had watched them every day. I watched their movements and the way they interacted. Prince Aeron was meant to be out on a late-night hunt, but when I arrived in the depths of night, there he was, laying in the bed, alone. Damien Knil was sat in an old oak chair next to a bed that was too large for the room, silently waiting for something unknown. He was watching the Prince sleep. It was like he was waiting for me to arrive, even though he could have never known I was there.

I used to do all my jobs dressed as a boy before I was strong enough to hold a glamour without concentrating. I was a different person when I left the institute to who I was reaching my job. It was important to go unnoticed and a girl looked much more out of place walking the streets than a boy.

When I went out on jobs, I became Clyde. Clyde with his slick back, onyx quiff. Clyde with his daunting eyes of ice. When he looked at you, you could feel your skin turn to frost. Clyde was just as short and nimble as Clydia, but wouldn't face being taunted for being out this late. Sometimes when I wasn't on a job, it was still easier to be Clyde.

I was making my way through the town to the far west. There are only a few houses this far out and they aren't owned by the rich. They're owned by the people the residents want away from them. It isn't very courteous, but unfortunately it happens.

It took me around a quarter of an hour to reach Damien's house. I knew he lived alone. Nobody else left the house and nobody came more than once. Other than Aeron. I don't know how they met. We're not even close to the capital.

It was well into the early hours of the morning when I decided to head out. My job had to be completed by the end of the day, so why not go and get a head start? I could rarely sleep back then so it made sense. As I was approaching the worn-down house, I noticed that there was a dim flicker in the upstairs window.

I didn't trust climbing up to the window. The wooden house was so old, it was bound to fall apart when I was halfway up. It would have been an absolute nightmare. I checked the front door. *Locked*. I knew there was a back door because I've seen both the boys in the lavender fields at the back of the house.

I walked around and twisted the back-door handle. *Also locked*. I knelt in the dirt and pulled out my lock picking kit. The moon was full that night, so there was just enough light for me to see what I was doing without having to test whether I could manage yet another thread of magic.

I listened for the tumblers in the lock to click, as I moved the pick up and down... *click*... one... *click*... two... *click*... three. A slight twist on the handle mixed with a bit of pressure on the door and I was in. I placed the pick safely back into the pouch I have for it in my sock and I closed the door silently behind me.

The back door opened into a small but tidy kitchen. There were pans hung overhead and a pot of utensils next to the cooker. I wiped my feet on the rotten welcome mat, I didn't want to be disrespectful, after all. In some houses I have even debated taking my shoes off just to feel a bit more hospitable.

I weaved my way through the kitchen and directly into a reception room. There was one lone oak chair that matched a small, round table. I wondered where the other chair was at the time and

I soon found out. The table was on an old red rug. It looked like it could be a tapestry hung in a palace if it were cared for properly. The kind you imagine the royal family to walk past every day and not take any notice.

Maybe it was a gift from Aeron?

To the right of the doorway coming off the kitchen there was a staircase leading to what I assumed would be the only room upstairs. I had already noticed a door to a bathroom on the other side of the kitchen, so it made sense. I was almost tiptoeing by the time I was halfway up the stairs.

This is why I prefer to climb up the outside of the house. A drainpipe or trellis will do. Makes for a less obvious entrance. Coming up through the house was a dangerous game to be playing.

I reached the top of the stairs and I was right in thinking that there was only one room, but it was much smaller than I first thought. I wondered why he had next to no room in here but then it occurred to me, there could be another door behind a secret bookcase. There were plenty of those in here.

I was surprised to see Damien awkwardly sitting in the other oak chair, extremely awake, long legs stretched out in front of him and arms crossed over his broad chest. I was even more surprised to see Prince Aeron asleep in his bed. I cleared my throat and Damien turned to face me slowly as I walked towards him.

My steps were slow but sure. I drew my knife out of its sheath and he knew then what I was here to do. Nobody should be this calm, especially when they have a dagger pointed at them.

My dagger has been my prize possession ever since Reagan gifted it to me. It has a nine-inch blade made of polished iron. The hilt is wrapped with dyed black leather. Including the blade, my dagger is only about twelve inches, but it's perfect.

I've never met somebody who accepted their death in the same way Damien did. His soft blonde locks looked darker in the low wash of light, but his blue eyes were as sharp as ever. They looked wise beyond his time.

'Aren't you scared?' I whispered as I reached him.

'Not at all. It's coming at some point and if I don't embrace it, then I have not lived my life to the fullest it can be. Sure I've had fun; I've felt things I didn't even know were possible. I have lived and that's all that matters. I am ready.' The words flowed out of him like he had rehearsed them a thousand times over.

'Do you want to say goodbye?' I nodded towards the sleeping prince, wishing a million times over I could have said goodbye to Reagan.

'I've said goodbye before and I've always come back to him, we've come back to each other. I don't want to say goodbye now with no promise of return. It's too permanent for this life.'

I've never admired anyone as much as I did Damien in that moment.

We both heard the gasp at the same time and turned to face the bed. It was only then did we realise how close we were to each other. Centimetres apart. If the prince hadn't seen my dagger before then he certainly did as we jumped apart, shock plastered across both our faces.

'I demand you tell me what is happening here, boy.' His voice was a harsh bellow in a sea of silence. He looked to my knife, then to Damien and then back at me. *He knew.* 'Who sent you? I must know.'

'I don't get the name, your Royal Highness. I just get given the job and a deadline.'

'When were you given this *job*?' He spat the words like a bad taste in his mouth.

'Last night, sir. But I always find it better to come when my target is asleep. It's far less painful for them.' *And for me.*

'What is your name?' he asked. I felt obliged to reply. Not just because he was my prince but because if I didn't, I was genuinely scared he would beat it out of me. His face was turning red with impatience the longer I didn't answer.

'My name is...Clydi...Clyde, sir.' He took my stumble as shock of meeting a royal over my forgetting that I was glamoured as Clyde.

'Well, Clyde, I suggest you scram before I march my personal guards over here to assassinate *you*.'

'Yes, your Royal Highness.' My voice was much smaller than his, despite the glamour.

'Clyde...' I turned to Damien, his voice hushed like he didn't want the prince to hear. 'Please, just do it.'

'I won't,' I responded as I turned to leave the room. I wanted to leave with my head held high and still attached to my shoulders.

He grabbed my arm gently and turned to the prince.

'Aeron, she has been sent here to kill me and I know it was by your father. How he found out about us I will never know, but we have to protect her.'

I swung my head to face him. '*Her?*'

'I can see through your glamour, sweetheart, and no boy kills with a dagger as dainty as yours. You don't have to tell me your name, but I would like you to do this as quickly and as painlessly as possible.'

Aeron was so angry he was spitting with almost every word. 'I won't let you do this, Damien. I love you. I'll speak to my father; everything will work out. He just doesn't understand what it is to love and be loved since Mother died.'

'Your life is full of potential, babe. You were born to command an army. I will never be accepted.

I'm an orphaned farmer's son that couldn't even maintain the land he was left.' Damien turned back to me. 'What will be the least painless?'

Prince Aeron was angry but he knew he couldn't change Damien's mind. *This was happening.* Damien was knowingly sacrificing his life so I could continue with mine. They both climbed into bed whilst I left the room so they could say everything that needed to be said.

I heard '*come in*' no more than a few minutes a later. It was a whisper, and I couldn't tell which man it had come from.

Aeron removed himself from the bed. 'I can't watch the life leave your eyes,' he said as he was beginning to stand. He strode out of the room with only one glance back to us as he was passing through the door frame. I waited until I heard him slam the front door shut before I turned back to Damien.

'Take this.' I handed him a flask filled with diluted foxglove oil. 'It'll knock you out before it happens.'

He gave the bottle a sniff. 'Is this foxglove? I swear this is poison!'

'It is, but it's diluted. The right amount acts as a therapeutic dose. It can slow your heart to put you into a deep sleep.' I said the words as gently as I could whilst maintaining an air of certainty so he would trust me.

He nodded once and threw his head back, meeting the flask with his lips. He swallowed the contents in just a couple of gulps and laid back down, wiping his mouth. 'How long until we get some action with this?'

'You'll be unconscious within a few minutes.'

I sat on the chair waiting for his eyes to drift shut. The candle was starting to burn low, so I gently blew on it to encourage the light to build back up. By the time I had gone to the bathroom he was asleep. I checked to see if he was still breathing. He was, but only slightly. I was glad he didn't have a reaction to the foxglove because they can be quite nasty to watch.

I slowly took my blade off the chair, I had placed it there before I wandered off. I didn't even realise I was at the bed until my knees brushed the mattress. His chest making small movements up and down made the reality of the situation hit home.

I did it quickly.

Damien's heart had stopped beating before I had even pulled the dagger out of his chest. He was still. He seemed peaceful. He deserved as much decency in death as he did in life. I pulled a thin blanket over him before I turned on my heel to leave.

***

The walk back to town passed by slowly. I walked through the fields just outside of the centre for hours. When I finally reached the institute, the sun was rising. I was exhausted but I had one last thing to do.

I walked up to my bed in the dorm and collected the few things that I owned. I saw Alex as I was walking down the stairs and grabbed her for one last hug.

'What's going on poppet?' she asked. A single tear trailed down my cheek as we broke apart. I turned without a word and continued my journey down the stairs, and straight out of the front door.

I do regret not saying goodbye to Alex but after that night, I knew I could never break up a family again. I could never do my job again.

I was alone. *Again.*

CHAPTER FIFTEEN
Adelaide

I'm going to quickly run you through the physics to magic concepts that went into this shield. It won't take long, but hopefully, you'll understand.

The prototype is all built and ready to go. The main part of the shield is iron, and the rest is mostly silver. Iron is much less conductive than silver, so you're less likely to be fried if a spell travels through.

The core is silver. That's one of the things I asked June to pick up yesterday. The silver core is unquestionably more conductive, so it'll be easy for magic to travel through thus the extended shield will be stronger, because the magic has used less energy to travel through the shield.

The other thing I asked June to pick up for me was a handle that had been wrapped in leather for comfort, and another layer against the frying of yourself. Remember that this is just a prototype and it will need to be cleaned up and properly fitted to the wizard who is wielding it before it's the best it can be.

The spell is the hardest part to generate, though. It has to travel through the silver core whilst storing the magic in a source which can be found just below it. It has to recognise the owner, too. If someone else used it, the magic would be drained. It could only be restored once the true owner projects through it again. If not, it's just a piece of metal that would do an okay job at taking hits.

The physics behind a forcefield is fairly simple to understand. You have to create a field of ionized, heated air. The plasma will disrupt the shock wave resulting in a force field.

The enchantment, on the other hand, is a bit more complicated.

Everyone's magic is individual. It is made up of a unique pattern of elements with varying amounts of earth, air, wind and fire. The spell I have created reads your magical fingerprint. It can tell how much of each element is present in your waves. I wish I could explain the magic system more but, to be honest, I don't even know.

You'll be able to see the difference when you cast a simple spell with the enchantment on you. The magic beacon for the spell is split. The red string is fire, the blue string is water, the green string is earth, and the remaining white will show us your level of air magic.

Once this has been read, it can be projected to the shield using *alliges duplicia elementum*. This will also bind your magic to this shield.

Once your magic has been stored into what I've been calling the memory, you can use *porro potentia* to extend it. I must warn you, though. The people using this shield have to be strong.

It has worked for all of us so far.

I have tested it for over an hour on every one of us and we could all bind our energy.

I've also created another spell to remove the memory, but I can't disclose that information to you now. All I can do is prepare in case it fails, but I'm sure it's going to work.

It has to work.

CHAPTER SIXTEEN
Florence

I'm not going to sit here and pretend that I'm not nervous about the next week or so because I am, but I also feel this strange sense of calm. Almost like this is my destiny and fate is calling me to take this chance. To make the move and stand up for what I think is right. For what *is* right.

We've decided to all sleep aboard the ship tonight so I needed to go back to our place and pack. I catch Addy just before we break from the group to go and get our things. She's fiddling with something on the prototype, but I honestly have no idea how it all works. She's a genius and I'm so proud of her for creating something extraordinary. I just know that this has to work with a mind like hers on the job.

'How are you feeling about all of this? I'm not going to lie; I am a bit nervous.'

'I think we all are,' she doesn't turn away from

what she's doing as she answers. I wonder if there's something really wrong for her to not even grant me the politeness of her full attention.

'I've been speaking to Ottie about how I'm feeling a lot,' she continues. 'And it is making me feel better. I just struggle to put it into words sometimes.'

I feel her on that one. I know how to speak to other people about how they're feeling, but dealing with my own emotions, that's a whole other story. I don't even hesitate before I answer.

'It's okay to feel like you shouldn't feel the way you do. I know it happens to me more often than I care to admit. Ottie is probably the bravest one of us. She has the courage of a lion, for goodness sake. She wants to protect you. It's what she's been doing her whole life. You're her baby sister.'

'I know.' She pauses before continuing her sentence. A look of frustration passes over her face. 'Now I bet you think I'm silly, too.'

'I'll never think you're silly. You feel the most out of all of us, and I appreciate that more than you'll ever understand.'

She reaches out and hugs me. 'Thank you, Flo. I really mean that from the bottom of my heart. Now, let's go and kick some royal butt with our magic and our smarts.'

'That sounds like a plan we should have started months ago.'

We both giggle like the children we are and I instantly feel lighter. I'm glad I could make someone feel better today.

Just as we both settle down, Dru wonders over to us and asks if I'm ready to head back and grab the things we need.

'Sure thing.' I focus my attention on Addy before we leave. 'I'm really proud of you, Ad. Catch you later.'

'Where did that sudden burst of emotion come from?' Dru and I are just clearing the forest path when she asks.

'We were just talking about how we felt about the next few days. She's worried people are going to get hurt which, you know, I do understand but like... every cause has sacrifices.'

'Are you worried about having to hurt anyone?' She raises her eyebrow at me in suspicion.

'I'm a natural born healer, and I have seen some sights over the years, but even a dead body is more than enough to freak me out.'

'You didn't answer my question.' *Damn, she's good.* I decide that it's best to answer as plainly as possible with Dru. She's basically my little sister at this point and she always knows when I'm lying.

'Yes.'

'Me, too.'

'We're brave, aren't we? We're fighting for all women. We're fighting for them and any sacrifices will be worth it. Plus, Clydia is around. She knows how to make it as painless as possible.'

'She does indeed.' Her voice is small. I look over at her and she's worrying at a hangnail on her thumb.

'How are you feeling about everything else?'

She stops for a moment to think before she continues on. We wander in silence until she's gathered her thoughts enough to speak them aloud. 'I think I'm feeling okay about it. As long as we get enough sleep.'

I chuckle under my breath at her response. 'We better not forget our tent then. Six days of sleeping under the stars in the middle of November doesn't sound too great.'

'I second that.'

She's about to say something else, but she throws her leg out in front of her and cries 'Aaaah! Flo help me!'

I turn to see two puncture wounds in her leg. I know she has worse words ready to spit out, but I can't be mad at her for that. I grab her before she falls to the ground and help her steady whilst I look for the snake. I see it just as it's beginning to disappear back into the woods.

It's a viper.

Venomous.

Deadly.

Drusilla is still swinging her leg up and

touching the bitten area. 'Flo, am I going to die? What kind of snake was that?' Mania and panic fill her voice. I know the venom will spread faster if she carries on this way.

'Okay for a start you need to calm down.' I take off my boots so I can get to my sock. She looks at me in disgust. 'I'm going to carry you back to ours. It should only be another ten or so minutes if I move quickly. Hold this against your bite and put pressure on it. Luckily, it's cold so that should slow the venom.'

'It was venomous? Flo, am I going to die? Am I going to...' she stops what she's saying to throw up. I don't know if it's from the venom or the adrenaline, but we have to move. I scoop her up and walk as quickly as I can with her legs dangling over my left arm. I watch her putting pressure on her bite with her right arm and feel her left slung around my neck. My right hand is supporting her lower back where she's slightly at an angle.

I'm strong but I don't know if I'm strong enough to make it all the way back with Drusilla hanging off me.

I can sense her focusing on trying to breathe whilst I'm running through a list of what I know I need to make the anti-venom.

A paste and a juice.

That should clear it up quickly.

Just two medicines.

We finally reach our home and I set her down just long enough to get the key and open the front door.

'Lay down on the dining table whilst I go and get what I need.' I think she's going to fall on her face as she's moving to the table, but she has her hand balanced on the wall for support.

I hear the wheezing as I'm rushing away from her. *That's not a good sign.*

This venom is acting faster than I expected. The bite must be deep enough to sink straight into her blood stream.

It takes me less than a minute to find what I need. I keep all sorts of things around the kitchen in case I ever need them. It's even handier that the plant for an antivenom medicine is right next to the door.

I grab some alcohol and a wet cloth before heading back over to the table. Her eyes are raw from crying and her breathing is unsteady.

'Dru you better stay with me. Damn it. Keep your spirit and your soul close to your body.'

The sock she was using to put pressure on the wound had fallen at the door when I put her down. The bite is aggressive. It's the colour of fire and covered in blood. I start by cleaning the blood off with the wet towel so I can see the puncture marks. They're clean, at least. That's a good start.

I extract the juice from the maka plant, not even

bothering to dilute it. I lift her to a sitting position and hold her upright as she takes the juice from my hand. She's just strong enough to tilt her head back to down the contents of the glass before handing it back to me and falling down onto the table. Her face is turned to the side and she's retching like she's going to throw up again. 'Keep it down, Dru, it'll help.' She moves her head in what I think is a nod.

At least she has an antidote on the inside whilst I'm working on extracting the paste.

There's an old wives' tale that if you extract the paste from the bulb of an onion, it acts as an antivenom for snake bites.

It takes a couple of minutes to get all of the paste out of the bulb and mashed in a bowl. *I feel bad for doing this already.* I give her something to bite on whilst I apply the alcohol to the wounds. 'This should stop any infection coming through,' I tell her. I'm sure she would have screamed if she had the strength. Instead her entire body tenses up and she starts sobbing again.

I wonder if this is more painful than actually getting bitten.

As soon as the alcohol has started to dry out, I apply the paste in a thick layer. The juice has started to kick in and the redness is softening already. Dru seems like she's in less pain, but she's still wheezing and has now started sweating, so I assume that something is hurting more than she's letting on.

I wonder if there are any spells that can speed the process up.

I know that *sana* is heal and I'd learnt the word for poison in a book. I just hope it was non-fiction and not a story.

I think the spell helps to contain the magic to one area until it can locate the source of the injury and burn it out.

'*Venenum sana.*' The words are barely a whisper. You have to feel confident when you're casting to make the magic stronger. I put on my bravest face and repeat the words.

'*Venenum sana!*'

Drusilla's body jolts up and back down. 'Dru?'

No response.

'Dru?' I want to shake her, to wake her, but she's burning up.

I hold myself up using the table and cast the spell one more time.

This is not the time for my sister to die.

CHAPTER SEVENTEEN
Florence

By some miracle, granted by the Goddess, Drusilla's eyes flutter open.

'Water...' Her voice is raspy but I'm happy that she's now regained consciousness. I basically throw the water at her. I want to cover her in it to cool her skin down, but instead I hand a full glass to her. She gulps it down and returns the glass to me, silently asking for more. I do as she asks.

'Slowly this time.' She takes the glass from my hand and sips. 'How are you feeling?'

'I'm not going to lie to you, Flo, I've felt a heck of a lot better.' There's my Dru, back to making light of a situation with her easy-going attitude.

'Try and sleep whilst I pack what we need. Is there anything in particular that you want?'

'I'm not going to turn down some sleep right now. I'm exhausted and I'm pretty sure I'm still dying.' She laughs to herself at that. I don't know if it's the magic or the remedies, but she seems slightly delirious. She looks at me with an intense gaze that I've never seen from her. I feel like she could read my darkest secrets with that stare. 'I trust you to pack what you think I'll need.'

She lays back down and is asleep almost instantly. *I'll need to find something to bandage that bite up.*

I leave Dru to her slumber until sunset. Her breathing has levelled out and the puncture marks are still clean. They're no longer ferociously red, so I assume all of the venom has been burnt out of her. Her skin is also back to a more normal temperature.

I sit and watch my sister for a moment before waking her.

She's beautiful. Her skin is a deep tan that makes me wonder whether her parents had been from different places, and her lashes are almost long enough to brush against her little poppet nose when her eyes are closed. I call it a poppet nose because it has a perfect little circle at the end. Although she has been sweating from the burning heat, her red hair still lays perfectly out to the sides next to her.

I gently shake her. 'Dru, honey, time to wake up.'

She slowly opens her eyes and pulls herself to a sitting position. 'What time is it?'

'The sun has just set and we're coming into

dusk.' She nods her understanding. 'How do you feel?'

'Surprisingly well. I just feel very tired.'

'I'm not surprised.'

We sit for another few minutes so Dru can get her bearings and I ask if she's ready for me to bandage up her leg.

'Can I change before you wrap me up? I feel disgusting in these clothes.'

'Sure, take your time.'

I think she's as keen to get out of this situation as I am.

Whilst she's upstairs, I start ripping a wash cloth into strips. She hurries back down in a clean black dress and hops up onto the table. 'I thought wearing a dress would be better for today, not rubbing the wound and all that.'

'Good idea, kid. You're getting too smart.' She flips her hair off her shoulders and swings her head to the side. *Good to know a near death experience hasn't taken her cheeky attitude.*

'Bandage me up please, nurse,' she jokes.

'If you could straighten your leg please, patient, I would be happy to apply this very complex medical device to your area of injury.' I say it in a fake lofty voice and we both start laughing as I tie up her bandage. 'Want to take it for a test drive?'

She walks back and forth across the kitchen a few times before stopping and looking slightly puzzled.

'Yes, I think I'll take enough for seven days.' It's difficult to keep a straight face around Dru at the best of times, but it's even harder when the adrenaline has worn off and you're both just out of control.

'Are you ready to grab that big bag of yours and wander to the ship?'

'Sure am.'

We load our bags onto our backs and I offer to carry the tent since she had enough to worry about today. I make sure I pack some food for tonight in a side bag and nod at Dru to signal that I'm ready.

We start the walk to the ship and it feels like a relief to be out of our house for a little while.

'I bet nothing on this journey will be as painful as a viper bite. I honestly thought I was going to die.'

'Me too, kid, but you didn't and you're in better working order than you were before. Just don't stand on any others and they won't bite you before you can lift your foot off.'

'Yes ma'am.'

***

'Where have you been? We're all so hungry,' Ottie moans elongating the last word of each sentence as we head up the ladder to the top deck.

'I'm sorry to inconvenience you. I was bitten by a very venomous snake and almost died, but not to worry, I have a selection of treats for this feast.'

'Stop messing around and give us the food.'

'I'm serious, I can show you. Do you think I'm wearing a dress in this weather for fun?'

'*What?* I didn't look at your leg. I'm sorry, Dru.' Ottie seems genuinely guilty, closing in on herself and becoming slightly awkward.

'I'll rewrap it for you once we've eaten,' I say. 'For now, let's start a fire in the pit. I have minced beef so we can have patties. I also have fresh bread, a knob of butter and a whole load of different cheeses. I even have brie.'

'Warm brie smoked over the fire with some fresh bread...mmm...the best.' Ottie looks like she's going to start drooling any second.

I drag the food over to the others as they start setting up the cooking area.

An hour later and we've all eaten. I'm ready to hit the hay but nobody makes a move and I'm not going to be the first one to break this moment. This six of us are snuggled under the night sky, full of food and ready for adventure.

I recognise popular constellations that my parents pointed out to me as a kid. *Orion. Delphinus. Ursa Major.*

The same constellations I have fond memories of are in the sky tonight. Coincidence? I think not.

It's destiny.

Slowly, the other girls start drifting off.

Dru and I are the last ones awake and we're whispering to each other about nothing. I don't know what I would do without her sometimes. She's the sister I never knew I wanted.

All of the girls are, really, but Dru and I have been together the longest.

And now we're going on our greatest adventure.

Together.

CHAPTER EIGHTEEN
Ottilie

I've only just woken up and I can hear the others shuffling around downstairs. I force my eyes open and the sky still has the pink tint of sunrise.

I wish whoever is making this much noise to stop but the banging continues. I sit up in defeat, accepting the loss of sleep. I rub my eyes, cough and stretch my arms up.

'Morning,' June's voice twinkles from behind me. I look around at who's left asleep and notice Dru a couple of paces away from me but that's it. We're the last two sleeping. I'm surprised that Addy is up, she hates mornings, but then again, she can never sleep properly when she's nervous.

'Morning. How is everyone getting on?' I stand up and stretch out some more muscles. My back aches from rolling over in the night and ending up on the floor.

'We're almost ready to set off. We wanted to let

you both sleep as long as we could. How are you feeling?'

'Honestly, I'm a bit nervous but the worst is yet to come, so let's take each day as it comes. I'll let myself be nervous on the day we go in.'

'Sometimes I think you're too mature to hang with us,' she sighs. 'Want some breakfast?'

'Always!'

Breakfast is delicious. It's such a treat from all of the plain food we've been eating recently. I pile a bit of everything on my plate. Bacon, scrambled eggs, potato and toasted bread with the remains of the butter and cheese.

Dru wakes up just as I'm finishing my eggs and grabs my last bite of cheesy toast. I feel like I'm going to snap but she almost died yesterday so I keep it to myself as she pops it into her mouth. She takes a sip of my orange juice. *I squeezed that myself.*

'Oi, squeeze your own if you want some,' I joke.

'I need the vitamins to make up for what I lost yesterday. The venom drained them all out of me.' She pretends to faint and I roll my eyes at her poor acting. This girl thinks she's a comedy genius.

'All right, all right. Take it. You owe me an orange juice.'

'On my heart do I swear to juice you the same number of oranges I am about to drink.'

The sun has completely risen when I run into town. I'm picking up the oranges Dru promised to juice as well as extras for the road. They're rarely in season here so they're expensive when you *can* get them. I haggle with the owner and get twelve for the price of ten before darting back to the others.

I get back to the ship and everyone has their bags next to the exit down to the dock, but I can't see the owners that match the luggage. *They must be downstairs.*

They're all hovering around an old table that holds a map of the Delgosi Isles.

'I think we should try and make it to at least Southmare today.' June is so optimistic. Of course she wants to make it straight to the next town, but everyone knows that Southmare is over a days' walk.

'Don't they have a dock too?' I ask.

'Oh hey, Ottie, when did you get back?' Flo turns at the sound of my voice and smiles at the bag full of oranges.

'Just a few minutes ago. But back to my question. Doesn't Southmare have a dock too?'

'Yeah, I think so, why?'

Perfect. We might make it there in time for me to make some money tonight after the price of those oranges.

'Let's go by sea. We have a rowing boat. It'll shave off hours of time because we won't have to go inland and then come back out.'

'One of us will definitely fall in,' says Dru, 'and that one of us will be me.'

'Addy, do you still have those weird neck things from when we all learnt how to swim?'

'Yeah, they're in my lab.'

'Perfect. You won't drown if you fall in then, Dru.'

She grunts but gives in to my obviously good idea. 'Okay fine.'

'Is everyone in then? Are we taking the boat?' I ask, looking around the table at my sisters.

There's silence around me until Addy speaks. 'I think it's a great idea. The wind is working in our favour today.' After some hesitation, agreements are made and we have a plan of action.

Now we just have to set off on the task of a lifetime.

Addy and I let everyone potter around downstairs in the warmth whilst we set up the boat. It doesn't take long before we're ready to board. Addy lowers the exit ladder and the rest of the coven flock downstairs. I wave at them from the top deck as I hoist the ladder back up and they wait for me to lower the boat down.

I turn the wheel of wire holding the boat tight against the side and it gradually makes its way down the ship.

'Another metre and you can stop,' I hear Addy shout. I sometimes forget how tall our ship is. *It does have seven floors.* I crank for what I think is the final metre and hear a gentle splash. *Perfectly done.*

I grab my backpack and start to scale down the side. There are plenty of ridges I can get my hands and feet into that act like a ladder on my way down. It only takes a couple of minutes before I'm in the dingy boat with everyone else.

'Nice job of that scaling,' Clydia comments, nodding her approval at my descent.

'Thanks, I learnt from the best,' I wink at her.

She's the one who taught me to climb a tree back when we had a look out for practise.

It seems like so long ago now.

Who would have thought two years ago that we would be making this journey together now?

Who would have even thought that six witches would have the confidence to meet, let alone show each other their strengths and weaknesses?

I unhook the boat from the big metal clips attaching it to the wire. They're a bit stiff but with a few cuss words and an attempt from everyone, we finally get them off.

Addy explains to us the most efficient way to row based on the wind speed and direction. I'm not really paying attention, my thoughts are bouncing around and my hands stinging from the rough metal hooks, so I just catch the end. 'If we stick to the coast line, the sea won't be strong enough to pull us out.'

'Everyone ready?' Flo asks. We nod and she starts the count to make sure we're all in sync.

When we're far enough out, we have to try and turn the boat to face south. It isn't easy considering none of us have any experience in a row boat, and we have the joint coordination of a stick.

'It's amazing that I can make myself disappear but we can't even turn a boat round without struggling.'

'I can make it burn from the inside if you would like?' Dru offers. 'Then we can swim all of the way to Southmare.'

I stop moaning and concentrate, finally getting us back on our way. The wind really is working in our favour because it takes next to no effort to get a consistent movement whilst we move our oars in circular motions. My hair is whipping me in the face and leaving little stinging sensations all over my cheeks.

The sun is barely setting by the time we reached Southmare. The dock is more heavily monitored than Eastfall, but once we prove that we're no threat, they let us straight through and into the town.

We decide to pitch a tent and stay in the surrounding woods for the first couple of nights; save what money we have for inns when we need them most. We find the entrance to the woods that would lead us back to Eastfall if we followed it for long enough, and pitch our tents about one hundred paces deep.

As soon as the tents are up, we get a small fire pit ready to light later this evening. We sit in the entrances of our tents and pick at small amounts of food. Nobody eats much because we know we can hunt something fresh for dinner in a couple of hours.

We're just chatting about what we might find out here when we hear a gunshot too nearby to be safe.

Every single one of us jumps.

'I'm going to investigate,' calls Clydia from the tent she's sharing with June.

'No, it's too dangerous!' I hear the panic in Flo's voice as she responds.

'I've been in more dangerous situations than this. Trust me.'

Before anyone can say another word, she's up and out of her tent.

I hear twigs crunching beneath her feet.

When she's out of ear shot, I climb out of our tent and try to follow her.

'Don't even think about it.' Addy attempts to pull me back.

'Don't worry, I'm going to use *invisibilia* so whoever is out there won't see me coming.'

'Using magic is even more dangerous. Get back inside.' She hisses the last words.

'Listen to your sister, Ottie. Please go back inside your tent.' Without even seeing her, I can picture the furrow in her brow and the fear in her eyes.

I wish I could listen to them but I won't leave Clydia out there alone. I walk until our ugly brown tents are out of sight. I walk until I spot someone in the distance.

I cast the spell, just in case.

Invisibilia.

'Witch!' I hear in awe from behind me. I turn around and I am face to face with a stranger. She has raven black hair, a sharp contrast to her ghostly skin. She's quite a bit taller than me, to the point where I have to look up at her to make eye contact. Her pupils are so big her entire iris is almost black, but I can see a small ring of grey around the outside.

'Who are you?' I flash back into reality as I ask the question.

'You don't need to know my name. Only that I am not your enemy.'

'Prove it.'

'I can't prove it, but I can promise.'

CHAPTER NINETEEN
Ottilie

I remember a time when Clydia taught us all how to hunt. It was the middle of winter and we were all freezing. I had more layers on than you could count and my hat was pulled all the way down over my ears. I have *no* idea where she got the gun, maybe it was hers? Either way she had this massive shot gun slung over her shoulder that looked much too big for her.

We were in the woods north of Eastfall, so it was likely we would be alone the whole time. Men don't tend to hunt here in fear of killing someone on the passing track. It was peaceful knowing we were close to our base but far enough away to not disturb anything.

'First of all,' she explained, 'you have to listen. *Really* listen. Some noises will be the rustle of leaves in the wind. Other noises will be a hard snap. We're listening for the hard snaps. Some snaps are more delicate than others. For example, a rabbit will barely make a noise. They will snap the smaller twigs but breeze over the larger ones. Deer, on the other hand, will be extremely easy to locate. They may be light footed but you'll soon know about it when they are near.'

As if on cue, there was a snap just ahead of us.

'Watch and learn.' Her voice reflected her usual overconfident attitude.

It was like watching a natural born hunter. Clydia slipped into a zone of complete silence. Every step she took was careful, calculated. She caught sight of whatever had made the noise and lifted the gun. Adjusting the butt to sit against her shoulder. She looked down the barrel carefully and tensed her finger on the trigger.

BANG!

The sound echoed all around us. There was a thud a few moments later when her prey had hit the ground. She opened the barrel and dropped the empty canister to the ground. She then slung the gun back over her shoulder and set off.

She motioned for us all to follow her over to her prey, and I was almost sick.

She shot a deer straight between the eyes.

'It's better to hit them through the head. The death is faster and much less painful than leaving them to bleed out through a hole in the stomach.' I was more scared of her than ever. 'Does anyone else want a go at tracking whilst I skin this girl and prepare her for dinner?' She drew a knife from her pocket and bent down to start shaving the doe.

Clydia's question was followed only by silence.

***

'Where are the others? I think my friend came looking for you.'

'We're around. We usually hunt in a group but I thought you might have been a big hit so I came out here. Turns out, you're a big hit in another sense of the word. Can I take you to meet them?'

'I really do need to find my friend.'

'We have the best tracker in Southmare, I'm sure she can find her if she hasn't already found us.'

Turns out, Clydia *had* already found them.

'Do you want to come back and meet our friends? We can hunt together. Flo can whip up a sweet rabbit stew.'

'I just hit a huge deer; in case you forgot the reason you came out looking for us,' the girl with black hair jokes. 'I hope she can do something with that.'

The group of hunting girls carry the deer back to where we have set up camp whilst Clydia and I lead the way.

'Hey girls,' I sing as we approach the tents. 'We have some guests for dinner tonight.' I've never seen Addy move so fast. She races out of the tent and swings her arms around me, pulling me into a hug so tight that I can barely breathe.

'Don't *ever* run to the sound of a gunshot again or I swear I will shoot you myself.'

'But *Clydia* can run to the sound of a gunshot?'

'Oh no she can't,' Flo replies from next to me. She's pulled herself out of her tent to give Clydia a smack.

'Hey, that hurt,' Clydia whines, rubbing the back of her head.

'Good.'

I turn around and everyone has awkwardly climbed out of their tents and are staring at our guests.

'These girls are like us,' explains Clydia.

'What do you mean? *Like us*' asks June.

'They weren't trying to hurt us when we heard the gun shot. They were hunting. Obviously, nobody knows they're out here or there would be consequences, but they are here now to have dinner with us.' Her voice is level as she speaks, waiting for somebody to fling an unpleasant response back at her. Instead, there are only silent stares.

'Oh, and they know that we're witches.' The look on everyone's faces is worth the thump I get from Addy.

'Well since they know, somebody start that fire and let's get this feast cooking,' chimes Flo.

Dru, obviously, loves to tease people so she stares at one of the girls, the one who had seen me disappear, and starts casting. She speaks the words *intus uri* and a flame bursts into life behind her.

She's getting too comfortable with that spell.

'Damn, nice job.' One of the girls from the other group admires Dru's work as the flames continue to dance. Her hair has been dyed a bright red that falls down to her bust. It compliments her pale green eyes. She moves forward and comes to stand in front of Dru.

'Rosalie,' she extends her hand, 'but you can call me Rosie.'

'Drusilla.' She takes her hand and shakes it politely, 'but you can call me Dru.'

'Well would you look at that. You do have names,' I dig at the others.

We all get introduced.

Robyn has long brown hair with matching brown eyes. She favours a hunting knife which she throws with perfect aim. She's the oldest, so she makes it her duty to protect the girls when they were out. She carries a small first aid kit strapped to her ankle, next to her knife holster. Her olive skin and the feline shape of her eyes makes her look like she could be from a whole other place.

Erin is an archer. Her short blonde hair is pinned back with a big clip and her blue eyes can catch the perfect bullseye. She has golden skin that's tanned from spending her days working out in the sun. Her arrows are finely made and she told me that she had designed and made them herself. Both the bow and her arrows are made from Osage orange which is, apparently, the most popular wood amongst archers. The feathers on the arrows come from turkey wings and the head is made from sharpened stone.

Carrie has bright white hair that matches her milky skin. Her eyes are wide and as red as blood, which is why they come out to hunt at night. If anyone in the village notices her, she'll be killed on sight. She won't even stand trial as a witch because they'll assume her red eyes are a sure sign. Her lack of vision means all of her other senses are amplified, making her a fantastic tracker.

Harper also has dyed red hair. It turns out she's Rosie's younger sister, so when Rosie dyed her hair red, Harper of course had to do the same. Looking at them now I can tell they're sisters, but rather than having pale green eyes, Harper's eyes are amber. A rare but sure sign of a witch. The only witch out of all six of them, but that doesn't matter. When she's around other people, she uses a glamour to make her eyes identical to Rosie's. They also have the same splattering of freckles across their noses which compliment their tanned skin. Honestly, they could be identical twins.

Last to introduce herself is Felicity, more commonly known as Flick. Her hair is as black as the night sky with single strands of white running through, like shooting stars making light in the dark. Her skin is predominantly brown but she has lighter patches dotted around. 'It's a condition,' she tells us all. 'There isn't enough pigment in these parts of my skin,' she points to the lighter areas, 'so they lose their colour and turn white.' Her deep brown eyes are a stark contrast to the white patches that circled them.

'I think it looks cool,' I reply, only sincerity in my voice.

They're more like us than I initially thought. These girls are an unlikely group of friends that found each other through a common interest. The only difference being that their interest is hunting, not magic.

'What brings you to Southmare if you're staying in a tent in the woods? Surely you can do that anywhere?' asks Robyn.

'We're actually on our way through to Fairpoint,' replies June.

'Wow that's quite the journey. Any reason you're going to the capital?'

'We have a plan,' I chime in. 'By the time we leave Fairpoint, you will be able to practise magic,' I nod to Harper, 'and you two won't have to hide your different appearances,' I gesture to Carrie and Flick.

Everyone is excited about what we're going to do as we spill each and every detail of our plan.

'You have big dreams, ladies. Are you sure you're going to achieve all of this in one go?' Erin asks.

'We know it won't be as full on as we hope, but a start is a start. If we can be seen as valuable witches, then we can be seen as valuable hunters and valuable blacksmiths.'

'I, for one, cannot cook to save my life so I have to hope that this works. I want to be able to go out and hunt. If I bring back the food, having put the work in, then my mother will never make me cook a single dinner again.'

'It's nice to see that you're so passionate about this, Flick,' I joke. 'Speaking of dinner, how is the food looking?'

'We're almost there,' Flo replies. 'Everyone grab a plate.'

There's a hustle and a bustle before we're all sat down with a plate full of food, and the noise makes way for the silence that comes with a group of people focussing on eating. The silence persists until June says what I'm sure we're all thinking. Well, I certainly am anyway.

'Would you like to come with us?'

The other girls exchange silent looks whilst we're waiting in suspense.

'Thank for the kind offer but we must decline on this occasion. Some of us have families to look after and others can't be seen out before dusk so it would make your journey much harder. With our whole hearts, we would love to be a part of what you stand for, in with the action of it all, but please know that we will be cheering from the side lines.' Rosie speaks the words in solemn tones.

We eat the rest of our meal in silence again. Not because we feel awkward, but because there are no words to say.

It's starting to fall into pitch black by the time we've finished eating and I offer to walk back into town with the girls. I want to get some work in tonight.

Best to take your victims money and move on without a trace.

'I'll come too,' offers Clydia. 'I want to see some of the town before we head off in the morning.'

'Okay sure, let's go.'

We say our goodbyes and leave with the promise of visiting them when we're on our way back through.

'We'll be back in a couple of hours,' I promise Addy as we set off, completely unaware of the events to come.

CHAPTER TWENTY
Ottilie

When we're halfway down the trail, I turn to Rosie and ask, 'where's the best tavern for gambling in these parts?'

'Oh, that would be the Cursed Sailor down by the docks.'

'What an enchanting name,' I joke.

'It's a lot nicer than it sounds. Come on, I'll show you the way.'

The other girls break off when we reach their routes home, and we exchanged pleasant farewells and promises to meet again someday. Even Harper takes off home, too tired to be tempted by a tavern. We continue the walk straight through town and down to the docks.

When we're nearing the docks, Rosie takes us down a side road with a sharp left turn.

The Cursed Sailor is a rough looking tavern on the outside. The brick was painted grey many years ago, but now there are enough stains on it to make it look abandoned. If it weren't for the loud cheers coming from inside, you'd think it was.

'Thanks for the guide here. I promise we'll stop by and see you on the way back. *If* we make it back.'

'Don't say things like that. Your ideas are brilliant and I know that you're going to come back in one piece.' She hugs me and throws a nod Clydia's way. She's already intuitive enough to know that Clydia isn't one for hugs, which is a great start for her. 'Good luck.'

'Thank you.' With those parting words, she leaves, taking the road back the way we came and away from the docks. We stand and watch until she disappears out of sight.

'Ready?' Clydia asks.

'Ready.'

We walk through the heavy doors and inside is simply beautiful. We're definitely out of place here. Everything is made of solid oak and covered in plush red velvet. The lighting is low and everyone is dressed well. Button down suits kind of dressed well. Unsurprisingly, there are no women in this tavern. *Can you even call it a tavern?* It's above the standard of any tavern I've been in.

'Blimey,' I hear Clydia breathe next to me.

'Yeah,' I agree, suddenly breathless.

Everyone turns to look at us as we enter. Whether it's because we're women or because we haven't washed since rowing here, I don't know, but people are staring.

'That table in the corner is free. Wanna sit there?' I nod towards the back corner.

'Sure thing. I'll go and get the drinks in.'

'See if they have some cards, too. I'm feeling lucky tonight!'

'You're always feeling lucky,' she chuckles. We move in opposite directions. Me towards the back to get our seat and Clydia towards the bar. Nobody here seems all that friendly, even though it's a nice place. *I guess the rich really are snotty.*

The seats are soft as I brush the velvet one way and back the other. I glance around the room and everyone has gone back to what they were doing, other than one man who is still staring at me. His blue eyes scolding me for just being here. His red hair is kept short, pushed back into a quiff. He looks oddly familiar. We hold eye contact, staring each other down, until Clydia slams two tankards of something onto the table.

'How did you manage that?' I ask as I scoop up some of the froth up with my finger.

'You just have to know what to say,' she replies throwing a pack of cards at me.

'What a perfect night.'

'Isn't it just.'

I shuffle the cards and get us ready for a game of blackjack, or twenty-one, if you want to call it that, with me as the dealer.

I stare into her eyes as I hit two cards down onto the table. Ace of hearts and four of spades.

'Hit me!' *The five of hearts.* 'Stick.'

I deal my own cards.

The queen of clubs hits the table first. *An ace to win on the first draw.* I take my second card. It hit the table and I look down. *The ace of spades.*

Relief washes over me. I'm a sore loser, which is why I make sure I always win.

'Cheat,' I hear Clydia hiss across the table.

'Sorry, love, dealer wins.' I wink at her and pass the cards over the table for her to shuffle.

I glance over at the man across from us and he's still staring. *What was his problem?*

Clydia taps the cards on the table a couple of times to both align the cards and get my attention.

She turns the top two cards over and looks me dead in the eye. A straight ace and ten. *Again.*

She chucks the cards back at me as I throw back my head in laughter. 'How? I shuffled them myself!'

'I'm an expert.'

We sip our drinks and chat about the new girls, hoping to meet them again someday. I can imagine us looking like one massive mob. A, first-rate group of girls. We could drop the coven label then too, I suppose, with only half of us being witches.

I place, well *slam,* my drink down slightly harder than expected and look over at that guy. *He's still watching us.*

'Hey, don't look now but that guy has been staring since we walked in.' She swings her head right away and he gives her a smile. It isn't a friendly smile, it's a malicious *I'm watching you* 'kind of smile.

'Stay here. I'm going to get us another drink and let the bar tender know to watch out.'

'Okay, hurry back.'

I try not to show my nervous energy but when he gets up and heads over here, I look in any other direction.

'Good game, kid. Why don't you show me how it's done?' he asks, pulling the cards towards him. He leans over the table and collects the two Clydia had thrown at me.

'Why don't you tell me your name first?' I try to sound surer of myself than I am.

'The name is Jake, Jake Brown. Who are you, stranger? You're not from this town. I would have recognised you if you were.'

'Jake Brown? Like Drusilla Brown? *I thought you looked familiar.*'

'I left that life behind when Drusilla ran away. Our whole family fell apart knowing we housed a witch. If you know her, I'm assuming you're a dirty witch too,' he spits the insult so aggressively that I have to fight my own anger to control my fists. 'Come on then, witch, let's play.'

'What are we playing?'

'Seems like blackjack is your favourite so hit me.'

'You have the cards. How about you hit me?'

'Fine. Let's get this over with before your little friend comes back.'

He shuffles the cards again. My heart is beating at the speed of light and I can hear the sound of it pushing its way through my thoughts, shifting my concentration. My palms are sweaty but I refuse to wipe them on my robe. *Why is he taking so long?* I glance at Clydia, who is still waiting to be served at the bar. When I look back my first two cards are already in play.

The six of hearts paired with the four of spades.

'Hit me.' I decide to glamour the card just to beat this wise guy. *The next card he turns over will be an ace.*

'Are you sure you want to do that?' he stares at me.

'Hit me.'

'Okay.' He draws a card and slaps it down onto the table.

'Check? Twenty-one. *I win.*'

'Actually, you're under arrest.'

'You're joking right?'

'Why would I joke around with a witch?' He sounds just as disgusted as he looks.

'Prove it.'

'I don't have to prove anything to you.'

I stand up and lean across the table. A tone harsher than I have ever heard escapes my mouth.

'Prove. It.' I think I look calm on the outside by my brain is whirring out of control.

'I took out all the aces,' he draws them from his pocket and fans them in his hands.

'So, you're a cheat?'

'No, I wanted to catch you using that glamour spell you think you're so good at.' He's practically steaming at the ears with frustration.

All I can think about is panicking.

I try to get away but he's too fast. I move to run but he shoots at me with *praeligo*. I fall to the floor with a thud as my legs are bound together. I manage to get my hands in front of me so I don't smack my face on the floor, but they're soon being pulled together behind my back.

Clydia came rushing back to me as soon as she heard my first frantic step but she's too late. I'm already bound on the floor and Jake is slinging me over his shoulder like I weigh nothing. I realise that I'm screaming and shifting, but my struggle only encourages the invisible bindings grow tighter.

'Get Dru!' I shout at her.

'What?'

'Get Drusilla. Now!'

They're the last words I manage to get out before Jake casts *altum somnum*.

The last thing I see is the panic in Clydia's eyes. A reflection of my own.

I try to look around, to find some help, but I can't even lift my head.

I let my body go limp as the world silences and everything turns black.

CHAPTER TWENTY-ONE
June

I'm in our tent getting ready to settle down and sleep when Clydia bursts into the middle of the campsite screaming.

'Help! Help! They have Ottie. Everyone wake up. Battle stations commence!' We all emerge from our tents at record speed.

'What's up?' asks Dru. Clydia is usually calm and collected but now she's frantic. I've never seen her behave this way.

'Jake is here and he's a *witch hunter*.'

'Are you joking?' Absolute dismay is plastered across her face. *Clearly not a good sign then.* She looks around. 'Where's Ottie?'

'He *has* Ottie. He caught her using a glamour. Get dressed. Come on!'

It takes us all a moment to process what she's said, but as soon as Drusilla starts moving, everyone starts moving.

Dru is ready first and waiting with Clydia. I can tell by the crunching of the leaves that she's bouncing from foot to foot just trying to stay warm. I hear their conversation as I'm sat silently tying my boots in the tent.

'Have you spoken to him?' Dru's voice is filled with sorrow. She had to walk away from her blood relatives once, and now one of them has taken a chosen family member.

'I didn't get a chance to say anything to him before I realised he was dragging Ottie away.'

'Oh…'

'He seems fine. He's well enough to arrest our friend and carry her through the town. He cast spells like it was no effort at all, too.'

'He's a wizard? He never told me.'

The tent is already open so I don't need to unzip it before clambering out. Flo appears out of her tent next, she's sharing with Dru, and Addy is last to emerge. She's tied her long, honey blonde hair back into a ponytail and secured with a thin black ribbon.

'Everyone ready?' I ask. I'm answered with a series of nods but there are no words. I know we're all worried about Ottie, but I've never seen this specific group of girls with no words, especially when it comes to a situation like this. 'Then Clydia, lead the way.'

She sets off at a sprint which she soon slows as we enter the town.

Clydia stops suddenly outside what looks like their local church. 'When I came to get you, they were coming through the back doors just to the right here.' She leads us around the side, and we find the back door. It's hitched open slightly. There's movement inside, and just enough space to peek through the crack in the door to the main hall of the church. The movement inside is coming from someone else. It isn't Jake or Ottie, it's some other guard with some other girl.

I look more closely. *Harper?*

Her angry red hair is the tell-tale sign. She's throwing herself around, trying to escape the invisible bonds that are on her. I catch her eye and she stills, little amber pools are looking back at me, pleading to get her out. *She can't use a glamour.* I nod my head once in slow motion. A *trust me* nod. She does.

I pull the girls into an alley next to the church so we're out of sight. My brain is working at one hundred miles per hour and I can tell Addy's is too. Everyone else just looks shocked. Even Clydia, who speaks so suddenly, I almost jump out of my skin. 'I don't understand. She was almost home when she broke off from us. Rosie assured me she would be safe because their house was just down the road from where the path split. I should have made sure she got home safely.'

Clydia rarely has a soft spot, so for her to be

feeling like this about Harper tells me the girl must have said something right.

I gently sit her down with her back to the wall. I don't think she even knows how she's feeling but that's okay. I just wish she had some kind of idea so I can talk with her, let this feeling pass, and have our best and only assassin back with us to help with what is now, essentially, a rescue mission.

I drop down next to her, and for some reason, the others followed suit. It holds this strange sense of unity. *I need to think. There has to be a clever way of getting both girls out of there.* Assuming Ottie is still in there.

Think, *think*, think!

'I'm going to do a lap of the church, you know, see what we're working with. Dru, do you want to come with me?'

'Sure.' Her answer is uneasy, the reality dawning on her that she hasn't seen her brother since she was sent away all those years ago. This isn't the time for uneasiness though. We're already one woman down, we can't take another hit.

'Okay good.' I turn to face the other three girls directly. 'Flo, Addy, stay here with Clydia. Make sure she's safe. See if you can get her talking.' At this point she's just sat in silence, staring. I know she feels like Ottie being witch-napped is her fault, she wasn't there. I know how this girls brain works and she's beating herself up right now.

'Yes ma'am,' they reply in unison.

I grab Drusilla's hand more forcefully than I intended to, but it helps her come back to herself a bit. She takes the lead, dragging me back around the church. This is a woman on a mission to save her sister, and her friend, from the enemy.

'You know, we should really start giving these missions names. Just so we don't get confused.' It baffles me how quickly her mind can jump from an absolute blank slate to suddenly being light and breezy.

I guess the shock of *probably* seeing her brother has worn off now.

'You think? Maybe we should,' I snort. *Someone has to keep the mood light*. 'Any ideas?'

'I'm thinking. There's something in my mind. It's on the tip of my tongue. I can taste the sweet victory that will be rescuing the girls and kicking evil butt.'

'You're so over dramatic,' I sigh.

'Well, now you don't get to know the mission name.'

'Fine, fine, fine. Tell me.

'Are you sure you're ready?'

'I'm ready to be part of this mission, Captain.'

'Ooooh, Captain, I like that.'

'Just get on with it.'

'The mission will be called...' she pauses for dramatic effect, but I'm ready to shake her to get it out.

'Operation: Our friend is an idiot and now we have to save her.'

I roll my eyes. 'A bit long winded isn't it?'

'Do you have any better ideas?'

'No, no, operation: our friend is an idiot and now we have to say her, it is.'

'Excellent.'

We're rounding the front of the church again when the front door swings open. It doesn't sound like it's safe to open it that violently. It sounds like the entire thing is going to fall. The door slams shut behind and I'm sure the entire church vibrates from the strength, but I don't have time to worry about that. Dru is pulling me into a bush before he sees us.

Jake.

He looks different to how I had pictured. I figured he would be a red head but those eyes, they could cut through the side of a mountain. Nothing like Dru's warm, welcoming brown.

We hold our breath to stop ourselves from laughing. I focus back on Jake, worried about losing him into the night, but he's just stood still. It's almost like he's waiting for someone. His red hair seems darker in the low light, and what was obviously a well put together quiff looking style before is now messy. I silently hope that Ottie was the one to mess up his perfect looking appearance as part of her revenge.

144

There's somebody I've never seen before approaching Jake. I look to Dru for confirmation but she shakes her head. 'Don't look at me, it's not my brother.' The new guy has shaggy blonde hair that curls to a stop above his ears. He's slightly taller than Jake and walks with a lot more confidence. They nod in way of a greeting, saying nothing.

Something about the situation doesn't seem right. Both men look around them to check that nobody had seen them together as they walk off, away from the town.

'I have a plan, providing he is going to be gone for at least half an hour. Can you keep watch here for a moment and hold the image of your brother as we just saw him in your mind? Glamour whilst I'm gone if you feel confident enough.'

I leave her there whilst I sprint back to the others. They're still huddled on the floor when I arrive, but Clydia seems to have evened out and is chatting to Florence and Addy.

'I have a plan. Are you all ready to begin Operation: Our friend is an idiot and now we have to save her?'

'Bit long, isn't it' Clydia asks, looking more confused than I did.

'Don't ask, it was Dru's idea.'

'Where is she anyway?'

'Oh, she's currently glamoured as her brother.'

'Right…' Flo starts uneasily. 'Want to explain?'

CHAPTER TWENTY-TWO
June

We're all in position when Drusilla, glamoured as
Jake, strolls in the front door. She waltzes in with
ease as she falls into a character she's known for so
long. Addy is waiting as lookout in the bush that I
left Dru in earlier. She knows the signal. I can only
just hear the exchanging of words inside the church.

'That was fast. Did the boss fire you or
something?' the other guy asks. He sounds closer to
the back off the hall. I peer through the crack in the
back door.

'Nah, he wants to see you at The Cursed Sailor.
He said to get there quick.'

'What about the *witches*?' He spits the last word,
like it leaves a sour taste in his mouth.

'I'll be here to watch them. You wanna anger the
boss?' He looks sheepish and Dru, or Jake, nods her
head in understanding. 'Didn't think so.'

He leaves quickly through the front door as we

enter in through the back. Drusilla flicks back into herself and starts untying Ottie immediately. She's only just coming round from *altum somnum*.

Dru and Flo focus on getting Ottie out of here whilst Clydia, Addy, and I untie Harper. It doesn't take long before we're getting ready to storm out of the back. Dru and Flo are just getting Ottie in a position to carry her back to the woods when the front doors come plummeting towards us.

Someone has blasted them off their hinges.

Jake?

The other guy?

The boss?

It's all three of them and they're flying at us. The buzz of magic encircling them.

The vibrations of powerful wizards filling the space between me and the next girl.

'Flo, Clydia, get those two out of here.' They grab a docile girl each and start carrying them towards the back door.

It slams shut and the boss bellows the words he would come to regret. 'You're not going anywhere.' He laughs. A dark, horrible laugh. The laugh of a villain in a fairy-tale. 'Seven little witches trapped here like prisoners,' the boss taunts. He's significantly taller than both Jake and the other guy, and has what I assume is long, mousey brown hair scraped back into a bun.

I watch Flo eye up the 'boss'.

'He may not be your brother, Dru,' says, dread filling her voice, 'but *he* is mine.'

'Hello little sister,' the boss chuckles. 'Long time no see.'

'Yeah, because you got my mother killed.'

'Don't you mean, *our* mother?'

'She was never *your* mother. She hated you. She knew you were trouble but your Dad wouldn't listen to her. Now look where that got him. In jail.' Flo's voice breaks with every word she speaks. She seems lost, the past she pushed down for so long suddenly rushing back.

'He deserves to be there for loving a woman who gave birth to a witch.'

'Wait, Flo, *you* have a brother?' Dru looks as confused as I feel.

'Step. Our parents got together just before I started displaying my powers. That's when Father Teddy helped me get away.'

'Oh, he's dead now by the way. We got to him before he could let any other witches escape. He told us you'd be here and he wasn't lying.'

'No no no...he wouldn't...you're lying.'

'Am I?'

He reaches into his pocket and pulls out the exact pendant Father Teddy used to wear around his neck. Gold with a small red heart in the middle. The sign of eternal love.

'He did lie to you, Felix. I've been living in

Eastfall all this time.'

'That doesn't matter. You're here now.' His dull grey eyes are staring at Florence and he's growling like an animal.

'Not for long,' she says, collecting herself. I watch her lips as she whispers '*interficio*' whilst staring at her brother. She has the control and she has the strength, but she has never practised this before.

I close my eyes and wait, hoping that I won't drop dead and I won't hear anyone next to me drop dead.

There's a succession of three smacks.

'Yes!' I scream as I open my eyes to see the men splayed on the floor. Empty looks in all of their eyes.

There's a fourth thud as Flo drops to the floor. Clydia and I rush to her, but the others stay where they are.

I hover my finger under Florence's nose to check that she's breathing. It's faint but I feel a small breeze caress my finger.

'She's breathing. Someone help.' Harper jets over and kneels down beside her.

'I know how to heal her but I can't guarantee that it'll be fast.'

'Just do whatever you can.'

'Okay, maybe go and deal with them,' she motions her head at the men, 'whilst I deal with this hero.'

Drusilla strides over to Jake, bends over, and closes his eyes, hiding a stare that's devoid of life. I forgot that she used to be close to her brothers. I make my way over to her when she drops to her knees and starts sobbing into Jake's chest. The part of his body that should be rising and falling as he slowly breathes in the scent of his sister is still. I feel bad for her, so I leave her to say goodbye to him.

I walk over to Felix and shut his eyes. I hate him, for Flo, but he still deserves some decency in death. I feel the same way about the other guy. He's dead and we never even knew his name.

He looks so peaceful in death.

The anger has melted from him and he seems somewhat relaxed.

I close his eyes, too.

I shift Felix in a more comfortable position and place the other guy next to him, all whilst reciting a quick prayer for the both of them before returning to Dru. She's still sobbing into her brother when I reach her. I loop my arm around her shoulders and she leans into me.

I look back to the others with a solemn glare which they returned with nothing but sincerity. The realisation of what had just happened hit me all at once. I pull Dru away from Jake and gently lead her back to Addy.

When Dru is safely through the back doors of

the church, I move Jake's lifeless body to lay comfortably next to the others. All three look like they're commanding troops in their sleep, like they could be standing to attention if they were up right. I take one last look at the bodies and make my way out of the back door to be with the others. They're all standing at the back doors waiting for us, waiting for *me*.

Harper is looking more shaken up than Ottie, but the worst of us is definitely Dru. It's the first day and we've already broken the no killing pact.

I don't want anyone to find the bodies and tie the murder back to us.

I don't want to do this but I receive a nod from Dru telling me that it's okay.

'Here lie the fallen,' I start. 'The fallen soldiers of the enemy.' It's harder to say those words than I expected. I want to use magic to give them a graceful send-off but Addy hands me an already lit match. It's quickly burning down to my fingers, but she holds eye contact as she speaks.

'Let's honour their wishes and leave magic out of this. They died at the hands of it.'

I suppose it makes sense to leave magic well alone whilst we send them off to wherever you go when you die. I hope it's a place with more witches than just us, and I hope they remember us, after all of this, so they respect them. I'm maybe too passionate about this right now but one small victory is still a victory. I place the match on a loose wooden panel, hanging down just above head height. It doesn't take long for the building to catch alight and for the people of the town to start taking notice. Nobody cares enough about the old church though, so we remain undisturbed.

We stay behind the church whilst it's still safe and we watch as it slowly starts to burn to ashes. The flames have reached the roof and it isn't long until it will, probably, cave in and crush all of us.

Dru takes a deep breath and says her final goodbyes to Jake where we stand. As does Flo with Felix. Both of them lost a family member today. Neither of them had seen in years, sure, but I know it stings. Losing anyone important to you stings your heart and soul.

We all agree that we're feeling exhausted so we drop Harper off home and make our way back to the forest. The trip takes longer than it usually would because Ottie's ankle is so swollen from her restraints that she can barely walk. Flo will definitely want to look at that when we're back.

'How are you feeling, Ottie?' I ask her.

'I've been better, but I've also been worse, so I guess I'm just at a steady level of emotional and physical pain.'

'Ah, well you're doing a good job of looking like you couldn't care less that you were just trapped by witch hunters.'

'Flo took them out pretty easily. It would have been cool to be aware enough of what was going on but you know, what can ya do?'

'She did look pretty dandy casting that spell in secret.'

'Dandy. I can't believe you just said *dandy*,' Ottie pokes after a couple of seconds.

'It's cool to say dandy.'

'I'm not sure you're right about that one.'

Leaving me with her bitter remark at my choice of language, she hobbles forward to talk to Addy.

I chuckle at her cussing when she puts too much weight on her sore ankle.

Considering the day we've had, I feel an odd sense of warmth. We experienced out first setback but we defeated the enemy.

We won.

Against all odds, *we won*.

CHAPTER TWENTY-THREE

June

We reach camp not long after. Everyone is shaking from the cold but adrenaline is still coursing through me. They all bundle their coats and cloaks on whilst I light the fire. We sit around not saying anything for a while, reflecting on what happened today.

Flo decides that she wants to cook something. 'A distraction from the intrusive thoughts,' she tells me. Florence is a carer, a healer. She certainly isn't a killer. I let her get on with it and I steal her spot next to Dru. She leans into me, still shaking despite there being two cloaks covering her from top to bottom. I throw my own over her and she curls in tighter. I hold her tight and look to the sky. Despite being so close to town, the night is clear. There isn't a single lick of smoke beyond our own, making the stars spattering the sky clearer than I've ever seen them. Staring at the stars makes it easy to forget about today. I tilt Dru's head up to join my gaze.

'What am I looking at?'

'You're looking at the stars,' I reply.

'I know that. I see them every night.'

'But tonight is special.'

'And why is tonight special?' She brings her gaze down to me but I lift her chin again.

'Because Jake is now one of those stars. He will always shine bright above you; he will always watch over you. He will always keep you safe and guide the way when you are lost. You'll know which one is him because he'll be the brightest one to you.' I feel her quickly wipe a tear from her face. Her breathing starts to grow shallow and she slings an arm into my lap. I grip her warm hand with my ice-cold fingers and she winces in surprise. She doesn't pull away, though, she squeezes my hand tight and leans her head on my shoulder.

'Do you really think people turn into stars?' Her voice is small, like a child who feels the weight of the world on their shoulders already.

'Do you?'

'I guess.'

'Which one do you think he is?'

'That one is the brightest.' Her finger is pointing directly above where we're sitting.

'I told you he would be watching over you.'

After another few minutes of silence and stargazing, food is ready and we all tuck in.

It doesn't feel like we had the same meal earlier in the day with new friends.

Positivity was surrounding us only a few hours ago, but the reality of how dangerous this is going to be is clear to all of us now. It's no longer the six of us, far away from wandering eyes. We're in plain sight and people are *mean*. They all want the reward for catching a witch. The praise from the royal family. The acknowledgement. *They want it.*

Silence fills the air as we eat. The only noise I can hear is the snap of burning firewood.

'Thank you for cooking, Flo, this is absolutely lovely, and my stomach feels happy,' Drusilla speaks softly.

'I second that,' Ottie agrees.

There's an onslaught of thanks passed over to Florence who, I think, is forgiven for the killing now. It had been necessary, and we all knew it.

'You're all welcome.'

I get up and squeeze her hand before collecting the plates ready to wash and pack away.

'Let me help you with that.' Dru jumps to her feet and collects the plates from Addy and Clydia, as well as bringing along her own. I gather the rest of the washing up, too. We wander away from the makeshift camp with everything piled high and an empty bucket swinging from my arm. Rosie had told us of a well that nobody uses, but is still filled with water, so we head there. We're far enough into the trees that all we have to do is walk north for about two hundred steps before I notice it in the distance and move faster.

I place the plates on the floor next to the well and Dru stacks hers on top. I fling the washcloths out of the bucket and they land on the stack of plates perfectly.

'Ugh I wish you would stop being good at that,' she jokes.

'Ugh I wish you didn't see me as such a hero.'

'Oh, just get on with it.' She rolls her eyes and chuckles at my lack of modesty.

I secure our bucket to the string using a touch of magic. The clip had broken off a long time ago and the ends of the rope are horrifically frayed. Dru takes charge and cranks the wheel, lowering the wooden bucket down,
> down,
>> down into the well.

It hits the water with a splash, and she keeps lowering until it fills with water. It's always heavier cranking the bucket back up, but Dru is strong and she takes on the extra weight with ease.

'Do you think anything else bad will happen to us?'

'I'm not sure. Bad things happen all the time but I'm sure if there is a bad thing it won't be nearly as bad as what happened today!' *I wish I could reassure her.*

'Okay.'

'Okay?'

'Yeah, okay.'

We never speak of our lives before, and she was younger than I was when she moved to Eastfall, so I can't imagine how difficult it was for her to process. The reason we don't speak about our past isn't just because it makes me sad, and I'm sure the others too, but because it's a time before we found people who accepted us. It was before we had a family who wanted us to achieve. It's funny, I find myself thinking about when I lived with my family sometimes, but they're never happy memories. I was always alone.

'What are you thinking about?' Dru asks.

I guess I've been quiet for longer than I thought. 'I'm thinking about my family before I met you guys. Before I had people who actually accepted me.'

'Wanna talk about it? Sometimes talking helps, you know, and it *is* your favourite thing to do.'

'They aren't happy thoughts.'

'Okay. What *do* you want to talk about?'

I have to stop and think for a moment. *What do I want to talk about?* 'Tell me a joke. I've missed your sense of humour today.'

'Let me think...'

We stand in silence, just washing the dishes, for a couple minutes. It doesn't take long because there aren't many but Dru is still thinking, so I let her continue swirling her cloth around the water uninterrupted.

'Why did the mages get lost?'

'Sorry?'

'The joke you asked me to tell. Why did the mages get lost?'

I take a second to think but the answer isn't immediately obvious so I give in. 'I don't know. Tell me.'

'Because they didn't know which was which.'

'*Oh, like witches.* Very good.' We stand laughing at her awful joke for a good two minutes, paying no notice to anything but the sound of one another cackling. As soon as we stop, it starts up again in a vicious cycle.

'Hey, do you mind if we stay a few minutes? I'm not quite ready to go back yet.'

'Sure thing. You want to talk about what happened today? About your brother? About any of it?'

'I don't think I'm ready to talk about any of it just yet.'

'Well, whenever you are, I am going to be here to listen.'

'Thank you.' The sincerity in her voice makes my heart hurt.

'It's okay. Now come on, let's sit and enjoy the quiet before we go back to the madness.'

We lay on the floor, not caring about the mud that would inevitably cover our clothes and hair.

159

'Do you see him up there?'

'Yeah, right there.' She raises her arm so it's vertical. There's a star that's brighter than the others right where she is pointing.

'I see him.' I raise my hand to join with hers. She takes my hand and lowers it, our fingers interlocking. Closing the space between us.

I turn to face her, and she gives me a sad smile. 'Thank you for being my sister. Thank you for being you. Just thank you.' Her words are soft and filled with love.

'We're like twins.' I nudge her and she giggles. She's usually full of life so it hurts to see her this sad.

We lay in silence, just holding hands. Her breathing is shallow but steady. I could listen to it all night because at least she's here, and she's alive.

'This has been my favourite mission so far,' I say to her, partially checking that she's awake because her eyes are closed.

'This is a mission?' Her voice is heavy, tired, but she's awake.

'Heck yeah it is.'

We stay there for a while longer, sharing whispered thoughts. 'Come on, lets walk back.' I pull myself up and grab her hand to bring her up with me. She isn't fully awake, so it takes her a moment to get her balance.

'You never told me the mission name,' she says

as we're picking up the clean plates.

'I didn't?' I pose it like a question.

'No.'

'Ah well. I guess you'll find out when you get moving so we can go back and sleep.' She starts walking faster as a joke, but I'm genuinely happy that we're moving. I just want to climb in my tent and sleep forever.

It's dark but I can still see with the fire of camp burning low. The others have already gone to bed, but Flo is still awake. There's a faint light coming from the tent she's sharing with Dru.

'She's worried. She thinks you hate her,' I tell Dru.

'Why would she think that?'

'Because she killed your brother.'

'Who was going to kill Ottie *and* Harper,' she speaks with certainty, like there's no question that Jake had to die.

'I know that, but I don't think *she* does.'

We separate from each other as we climb into our tents. I turn to her just before she zips hers up.

'Operation: Starlight,' I murmur.

'What?'

'The name of our mission tonight.'

She smiles at me as she draws the tent zip round. I hear her mutter something to Flo, but I can't make out what.

I thought Clydia was already asleep, but she

161

speaks gently when I clamber over her. 'What's the plan for tomorrow?'

'I guess we can figure that out in the morning.'

'You're right. I'm exhausted. I just wanted to make sure you were home safe before I went to sleep.'

'I love you.'

I don't think she hears me before her breathing levels out and she's asleep. I listen to her gentle snores. *She's alive.*

'Operation: Starlight,' I mumble to myself, 'is complete.'

CHAPTER TWENTY-FOUR
Drusilla

My eyes jump open, worrying about the events of yesterday. It takes me a moment to realise that it's still dark out and Flo is sleeping next to me. I assume I'm the first awake, so I decide to get breakfast started. I know we have the ingredients for pancakes, so pancakes is what I'm going to make. I think everyone needs a pick me up this morning and nothing can cheer you up like pancakes for breakfast.

June is next to wake. She stumbles out of her tent with as much grace as a baby hippo and plants herself on the closest log to the frying pan. 'Hey, I've got this,' I say to her.

'You sure?' She's already moving over, before I've even answered. Sleep still fills her comforting eyes as she yawns. *She must have literally just woken up.* 'Would you like me to make the tea?'

'Please.'

By the time June is back from getting fresh

water for the tea, everyone other than Ottie is awake. 'She really does like to sleep in,' I joke with Addy.

'She always has. It's like she falls into her dreams and forgets they aren't real.' Addy only just finishes her sentence when a scream comes from the tent she shares with her sister. She jumps into action instantly and almost trips over the log she was sat on moments before as she makes a beeline for Ottie.

After a minute or two of frantic mumbles and sobs, Ottie emerges from the tent with Addy.

'I had a dream about yesterday,' she announces. 'I dreamt of Jake.'

I tense at the sound of his name. I'm still not ready to accept what happened yesterday.

'You're safe with us for now,' I tell her when I've found my words. 'We're going to stick together. We're not going to leave any woman alone until we're safely at Fairpoint. I can't promise it, but I believe that if we all stick together, we'll be safe.'

'I like that you make no promises, Dru. It means nobody can be let down.' Her voice is still low, still sad, but she seems to have perked up a little.

'I might let you down in life, even without promises made, but what I won't do is make an awful pancake.' I plate her up a stack of four and hand her the sugar. 'I promise to always make the best pancakes you have ever tasted.'

'I'll hold you to that.'

She covers the pancakes in sugar. We all wait in suspense as she takes the first bite. She chews with an analytical look on her face, like she's a professional chef ready to give feedback. She swallows gently and smiles. 'Well, Chef Drusilla, this has to be the most *spectacularly delicious* pancake I have ever had the great *privilege* of putting in my mouth.' She over-exaggerates the words and I can't help but laugh at her good humour.

'I'm glad to hear it.'

'I highly suggest that each and every one of you try some of these delicious pancakes before I eat them all.'

And with that, breakfast is underway.

Everyone is enjoying their pancakes so much that I have to practically beg them to leave me at least one. I've only just perched back on my log with my singular pancake when Ottie asks, 'so what's the plan for today?'

'Well that depends on how everyone is feeling,' June replies, placing her empty plate next to her feet.

'I'm not going to lie to you, I've felt better.' Those words come from Flo who would usually let us decide amongst ourselves. If she openly says that she isn't feeling too great then something is really wrong.

'Are you okay?' I ask, trying not to sound as concerned as I am.

'Yeah, I'm just not feeling so good. My brain doesn't seem to want to work properly and I'm not sure how far I'll make it if we're travelling all day.' *I'm pretty sure most of us are feeling that way this morning.*

'The closest town is just half a day's walk.' June is the only one who seems ready to do this today if I'm honest.

'Sure.'

'We'll take it easy for a bit this morning and then set off around midday. We'll be there by this evening since it's just one straight road out of town.'

'Okay, June.' I don't mean to sound rude, but I do, and that's not how I want to start the day. 'Sorry, I'm just not doing so great either.'

'I understand. I'm pretty sure we all do,' there's a succession of nods. 'But if we don't keep moving then all this planning, all these sacrifices, they will have been for nothing. Yesterday wasn't in vain. It was the first stand and we all made it through. We are one team. We are together. We are *family*.'

I gently push her. 'Gosh, you're always so dramatic about it.'

Clydia gathers up the plates and pans ready for washing. Everyone heads to the well with her, arms piled high, expect for Flo and I. We climb back into our tent and lay there, just holding each other. Not in a romantic way, but in a *'we've got each other and it's going to be okay'* kind of way. We just want to protect one another from whatever is about to come our way.

Florence turns on her side to face me and lets go of my hand so she can tuck hers underneath her head. She slowly closes her eyes like she isn't ready to be awake, like she doesn't want to be part of this world today.

'Flo, can I ask you something?'

'Mhm.'

I'm not convinced she's fully aware of what I'm saying but I want to ask anyway. 'I would really like to forget about yesterday. I would like to forget about my previous life completely, if I'm honest with you.' She doesn't let me finish.

'Don't we all.'

'I wanted to ask, if it's okay, since you're my real family now and all, if it might be okay for me to go as Drusilla Flynn from now on?'

Her eyes spring open and I can see tears forming. The glossing it causes makes her greyish eyes look glassy. She doesn't answer my question, she just grabs my arm and pulls me into a tight hug, sobbing into my shoulder. 'Is that a yes?'

'I've felt lost for so long not having anyone that shared my last name. I know it doesn't make a real family, but it labels the people who are in it as one.'

'I don't understand. Is that a yes, Florence Flynn? May I identify myself as being one extra member of the Flynn family with you?' My heart is beating at the speed of light waiting for a definite response.

'Of course it's a yes. Welcome to the family, *officially*, Drusilla Flynn.'

***

'Right, have we definitely got everything?'

'Flo, can you see anything on the floor? We're staying in tents which have been packed away in our bags. It's not like anything has been accidentally kicked under the bed,' I joke, the bitterness of the morning is reflected in my unnecessarily mean response.

'Okay, okay. I just wanted to check. You'll soon be upset if we leave the frying pan behind.'

'Oh, you mean the frying pan that is in *my* bag?'

'You're such a know it all sometimes.'

I can tell that she's getting impatient and just wants to get on the road. It's approaching midday and if we don't start moving soon, we won't get to our next stop until late evening. 'We've got everything and we're ready to go,' I assure her.

'Right ladies, on to Madding Valley.'

We start at a good pace but within a couple of hours we're slowing down. Nobody has the motivation to continue today. Even June is beginning to slack.

'Let's play a game,' I suggest.

'Like what?' Ottie asks, swinging her arms to keep pace.

'Have you ever played *'would you rather'*?'

'Nope, sounds boring though.'

'Oh, trust me, it's not. Somebody comes up with two scenarios and everyone else has to say which they would rather do?'

'Boring!'

I roll my eyes at her lack of acceptance. 'Just give it a try. I'll go first.'

I take a moment to think. There's nothing worse than starting the game with an awful *would you rather*.

'See, even you can't think of one.'

'Give me a minute.' I take a few more seconds. 'Okay. Got one.' I clear my throat to get everyone's attention. 'Would you rather: drink the water that Ottie washes her dirty little feet in or eat a rabbit cooked with the fur still on? You have to eat the fur with it like it's seasoning.'

'Ew, Dru, why do you have to be so disgusting?' *Addy is as enthusiastic as ever then.*

'That's the point, you pick gross things because it makes it harder to decide which you would rather do. I thought it was simple.'

'Well, I for one wouldn't go anywhere near Ottie's foot water. We've all smelt her feet. So, it looks like I'm getting ready pick fur out of my teeth.'

'I like your thinking, Clydia, and I would definitely join you on this fur filled journey,' I agree.

'I'll drink your toe water, don't you worry.' Addy nudges Ottie and laughs. A high pitch song escaping her throat.

'I wouldn't even drink that water myself.'

'Flo?' I ask. June jumps in quick, never wanting to be the last to answer in fear that she'll be seen as following the crowd.

'I'll split that water with you, Addy. I can't think of anything worse than picking fur out of my teeth for three weeks straight. Imagine the fur balls too. That's nasty.'

'I hope the rabbit is big enough for four because we would definitely get some kind of disease drinking that water,' Flo contributes, a disgusted face followed by a vomiting noise with her response.

Ottie looks like she's taking it to heart a bit more than expected. 'Hey, they're not that bad.'

'They're not. It's just a joke, you loser.' I laugh, trying to keep my voice light in an attempt to reassure her that it's all just a bit of fun.

'Alright, I believe you this one time.'

'Right, who's next?'

We each take it in turns to come up with even more disgusting *would you rather* questions. A personal favourite is Addy's contribution of *would you rather eat a live worm or a live grasshopper?* She tries to play along but she just isn't as utterly disgusting as the rest of us. Someone here needs to have a bit of decency, I guess.

In case you wondered, we all chose a live worm. Imagine the crunch of a grasshopper. It sounds like a nightmare.

By the time we're bored of playing, we've been walking for almost two hours.

Playing games passes the time, for sure, but we've definitely exhausted *'would you rather'* for today. *'I-spy'* will consist of just trees and dirt, and none of us have the concentration to play the *'I went on a picnic'* game. The only other journey game I know how to play is twenty questions, and that's only because my brothers and I used to play when we were going to visit our grandparents.

'Can we play another game?' Ottie asks. I look over at her, surprised by her willingness to participate. Her green eyes are usually a reflection of a forest in the summer but today they look as tired as the trees of winter.

'What kind of game?' We seem to be the only people interested in playing anymore so I guess it's down to us to decide.

'I like twenty questions. If you know how to play that?'

'Of course I do.'

'I'll go first. Let me think of one for a second.'

'Don't take too long or I'll get bored waiting.'

'Well you can pipe down because I've thought of one already.'

I mock what she says in a childish, squeaky voice just to get her riled up again.

'Just shut up and guess.'

'Okay, okay. Are you a human?'

'Yes.'

'Are you alive?'

'Yes.'

'That makes it easier then.' I roll my eyes for the millionth time this journey already. We all seem to be in the habit of rolling at our eyes at one another.

After a few more questions I discover that it's a female that we know, but it isn't one of us. They also have red hair so that makes it either Harper or Rosie.

'Does she have an older sister?'

'No.'

'Easy. The person you are thinking of is Rosie.'

'I tried to make the first round easy, okay?'

'Yeah, yeah. Just because I got it in eight questions.'

'Fine, if you're so good then it's your turn!'

'Well I've got one already so shoot.'

'Fine. Is it human?' Ottie repeats my own question back to me.

'Nope.'

'Oh, come on... that's way harder than mine.'

'Well, it *is* in the rules.'

'Play fair, Dru,' June calls back to us.

'It's in the rules,' I shout at the top of my lungs.

'Not anymore. Now it has to be a person.'

'You're no fun.'

'Just pick someone new,' Ottie pushes.

I don't want to play with these new, boring rules, but it makes the time pass so we continue. It feels like we've been playing for hours before we give up and walk in silence, arms linked, ready to finish our journey and crash for the night.

CHAPTER TWENTY-FIVE
Drusilla

'Do you guys see the Lily Blue Inn?' Flo asks. I'm finally excited for a full night's rest in an actual bed.

'I can see the same things as you.'

'Look, we're all tired Dru but there is no need to act like that.' *June can pipe down as well.*

'I'm sorry. Let's keep walking. It's got to be in this town somewhere.'

We walk around and around so many little roads. This town is meant to be small, but it feels like a maze.

'There!' Addy's voice comes as a burst from the silence. 'It doesn't look very open, though.'

She's right. As we approach the beaten old sign, it's made apparent that there's no way we will be sleeping in the Lily Blue Inn tonight. I'm getting ready to just lay down on the floor and sleep wherever I fall.

'Well, I guess we're camping for another night

then.' Addy sighs.

'I was considering just laying down here and seeing how we get on.'

'Good idea, I'll join you on the floor.'

Just as we're beginning to make the jokes a reality, there's a clattering of hooves against the loose stones. A horse and carriage nears and draws to a halt, to which a grizzly man jumps out. He's tall and broad. His hair is darker than the night sky and his voice is low. 'Oh you've got to be kidding me? When did this happen? *Charles*!'

'I don't know when this happened, sire, but I can take a quick look around town to see if there are any other places to stay.'

The man who answered, Charles, is slight. He looks like a only slightly younger copy of Father Teddy. He shouldn't be walking around anywhere alone.

'Hello sir,' June says politely. 'We're also looking for a place to stay tonight. This is where we were hoping to rest before we continue our journey to Fairpoint. Would you mind if a couple of us join you on your search for somewhere to sleep?'

He looks towards the other man. *Obviously a helping hand*. The rich man nods to Charles, and Charles nods to June. 'You may come, and one other girl. The rest must stay here.'

'Addy, do you want to come and find somewhere to sleep? You're the most resourceful and creative.'

'Sure thing. Ottie, can you look after my bag?'

'Yeah, chuck it here.'

'Thanks.' She slings her bag across the floor. It hits Ottie in the shin before she slips it behind her.

Addy looks back at the four of us, still waiting with this stranger, and spares us an *'I'm sorry'* kind of glance. She might be sorry, but she still turns to face the right direction and continues at the same pace as June and Charles. Considering how old Charles looks, he can't half walk quickly.

Once they're out of sight, I extended my hand to the other stranger. 'Drusilla Flynn, pleasure to meet you.'

He grunts in response.

Rude.

Clydia and Ottie are shocked at my choice of last name but Flo and I soon fill them in on my reason. I also don't want to be associated with Jake, so it helps with that too.

The man sounds like he's about to choke up with tears. He finally extends us the courtesy of his name, but it's a whisper none of us hear.

Clydia holds out her hand next. She has a mean handshake on her when she wants to get some answers. 'Clydia Tam, nice to meet you. Can I ask your name?'

This big man suddenly looks shy, gentle. His black hair starts to lighten, his eyes start to shift from a deep brown to a soft gold, and his warm, tan skin suddenly splatters with delicate little freckles. Where the rather hostile looking man once stood, there's now honey blonde royalty. His voice is still deep, but it's light enough to know that he'd sung the words a thousand times. I have to steady myself when I realise who is standing in front of me. It's him. It's *really* him.

'Pleasure to meet you Miss Tam, Miss Flynn. I am terribly sorry I don't know your names.' He looks toward Flo and Ottie.

'Your highness, I'm Florence Flynn and this is Ottilie Lambert.'

'I can speak for myself, Flo.' She turns to the prince. 'Sorry, I'm Ottilie but you can call me Ottie.'

'Pleasure to meet you Ottie, Miss Flynn, *again*. Sorry, rude of me not to introduce myself. I'm Prince Laurence Griffin, but you can just call me Laurie.' He winks at Ottie as he makes the same announcement as her. 'Do you know what, I actually hate being called Laurie. My mum used to call me it and it makes me feel like a child. Maybe just call me Laurence.'

Breathe, Drusilla, breathe. My brain is already running at one hundred miles an hour knowing that my name has passed over the prince's lips. *Play it cool.*

'Well Laurence,' I tease, 'I can't wait for our little sleepover this evening.' He takes my right hand

177

carefully and brings it up to his mouth.

'Oh, neither can I, Miss Drusilla, neither can I.'

CHAPTER TWENTY-SIX
Drusilla

'This looks like a good spot,' Flo says, kicking at the ground. 'Not too far away from the town but far enough that we shouldn't be disturbed.'

Laurence looks like he's just seen a ghost. 'Yeah this looks great, but what about Larry?'

'Who the heck is Larry?' Someone had to ask. I'm just glad it's Ottie and not me.

'Larry is that majestic white stallion you saw pulling Charles and I earlier.'

'Well,' Addy starts, 'I could make him somewhere to sleep out of twigs and grass. Give me ten minutes and Larry will have a bed as luxurious as his in the stable of the palace.' She's practically bouncing with excitement at the thought of being able to create something.

'I'll hold you to that.'

Night is drawing in fast and Charles, who has recently returned with no luck, has just sparked a fire to life.

'How the heck did you do that?' June asks, obviously still frustrated that she couldn't start one last time.

'When you're the helping hand of the future king you need to know a great number of things. Knowing how to start a fire when your inn has closed down and you're having to sleep in the woods with a bunch of strange girls who, might I point out, could murder the prince at any point is one of those things.'

'You know, I *am* a trained assassin,' Clydia chimes in. 'I'll be able to protect you little princeling.'

'Do not speak to your future king like that.' *Fab, we've upset Charles already.*

The prince's soothing voice lulls the conversation. 'Charles, don't worry about me. I'm sure Miss Tam has no intention of committing treason tonight. They seem to have their own agenda.'

'Even more cause for concern.' *Charles really doesn't trust us not to kill the prince.*

'If it makes you feel better I will sleep in the carriage with you, but I was looking forward to spending time under the stars.'

After some back and forth between Charles and Laurence, the prince agrees to sleep in the carriage.

'I'm going to stay out until midnight so I can see

all the stars in the sky,' Laurence teases.

'You are your own person, sire, and can do what you wish, but remember that it is also my responsibility to keep you safe.'

'You're the best, Charles.' He swings him a high-five. *Fighting to spend time with commoners and high-fiving the staff. Is this the real price?*

Being the prince, Laurence has some pretty exquisite food to cook up. *There's so much cheese.* There are sweets for after dinner that I can only dream of having the money to buy.

We opt for cheese sandwiches that we cover in fresh butter and toast them. Pretty standard, our usual meals consist of something similar. Only this time, there is an extraordinary amount of cheese, and the other components are made with much more exquisite ingredients. I pull my sandwich apart and the strings of cheese between each half are thicker than the bread. I burn the tip of my tongue on my first bite and wince away from the meal, but it's so rich in flavour that I can't stop myself going straight back in for a second. I finish mine so quickly that Flo doesn't even have hers yet, it's still sizzling in the pan.

I wait for everyone to finish before I direct a keen look and a nod at Ottie. She knows what I want because she wants the exact same thing. We pounce towards Charles who is, unluckily, sat next to the box of pastries. The look on his face is one of pure terror. *He definitely thinks we're about to kill him.*

We grab the basket of pastries and snatch them toward us, laughing as his face relaxes before switching straight to a scolding glare. 'Calm down girls, those pastries have got to last the next few days. No other bakery in the kingdom makes them like this.'

I look directly at him and lift an apple strudel up to my mouth. I wink at him as I take a bite and he grunts as the pastry flakes drift down my front. I close my eyes and chew, taking in every single flavour. The apple is sweet yet bitter, the cinnamon gives it a hint of heat, the lemon enhances the bitter taste and the pastry is so buttery it practically melts in my mouth. It's like eating a little bit of perfectly crisp and golden-brown heaven.

'So good, right.' The price is grinning at my reaction. A Cheshire gin that reaches from one ear to the other. A grin that only someone full of life can bear. A chuckle almost escapes his lips. *Almost.*

'Yeah, really good. So good I think everyone should have one.' I start handing them out, beginning with Flo. She got her toasted cheese sandwich last so she should have dessert first. She picks a cherry Bakewell off the top and we stare as she unwraps it slowly.

'Right, you can all stop watching me and eat your own,' she snaps. I head around the circle, skipping Ottie since she savagely attacked one at the same time I did. I pop another blueberry pastry between my lips and hold it there using my teeth before handing the basket to Laurence. He feigns a look of upset before graciously taking the basket from my hand.

'You're so kind, Miss, how will I ever repay you for eating *my* pastries.'

'No need to worry about that, your highness, serving you is enough.'

'Aren't you a doting subject. If only everyone could be like you.'

'Just eat your pastry. What is it that Clydia called you? *Princeling*?'

'Ouch,' he flings himself backward and places his hand over his chest, pretending that he's been shot through the heart. 'What brings you to my great city anyway?'

'Well since you asked so nicely. We were actually hoping to get an audience with the king, your father, to show him something great that Addy invented.' He turns towards Addy at the mention of her name.

'What did you invent, Adelaide? Maybe I can help with that.'

Addy starts to tell Laurence about the shield, explaining how it works, when he stops her.

'You're witches, aren't you?'

'Sorry what?'

'Your determination. No person, that I've ever

met anyway, has near the amount of determination as a witch. You six have more determination than any group of people that I've ever met.'

'Sorry princeling but you're wrong this time.' Clydia tenses at the announcement. She's always the best at not being discovered, and if she is, then she's also the best at covering it up.

'Tell me how you've tested this shield if nobody knows you've made it, and you're not witches?'

Even June pauses now. The girl who has everything to say is speechless. Laurence would be impressed if he knew.

'So, are you witches or not?'

'How do you feel about witches?' Ottie asks.

'Honestly, I think they're pretty cool. Having magic is the best.'

'Yeah, it is,' she agrees.

'Aha, I knew it! I could have you killed where you stand.'

'Are you going to?'

'Going to what?'

'Have us killed where we stand? Well, *sit.*' She emphasises that last part.

'I don't think I will, no. I actually find you all quite interesting.'

'You better not be lying,' Clydia threatens, waving her fist around. 'Don't forget that I can kill you easily in more ways than one.'

He looks at Clydia with a challenging glare,

right eyebrow raised, and then back to Addy. 'Please do continue telling me about your shield. You're extraordinary.' She continues to talk to Laurence about the work she's done, and how she managed to combine both science and magic to make one shield. I'm impressed at how easily she's keeping him invested in our project.

***

Addy actually goes off to bed first. Closely followed by Flo, Ottie and June. Soon it's just me, Clydia, Laurence and Charles in the open air, but I can see that Charles is ready to go, too. Laurence dismisses him and he looks eternally grateful for the chance at rest. 'I won't be long,' he promises as Charles disappears into the carriage. I hear him snoring within a couple of minutes and it really makes me laugh. So much so, that Clydia and Laurence pause their conversation just to look at me.

I attempt to quiet my laugher but the harder I try, the more I cackle. I point at the carriage so they would both listen, but I don't think they get my gist. By the time I have myself back under control, the snoring has stopped and they've continued on their conversation. *I wish I knew what they were talking about.* A few minutes later, Clydia says her goodbyes and heads off to her tent, where June is already sound asleep. It's now just the prince and I alone under the night sky.

I move to sit with my back against the carriage and lift my knees to my chest. I can feel my long hair being tugged against the wood as I wiggle my head around. Laurence shifts over to sit next to me, his back in line with me. Our shoulders are touching and we sit like that, together, in silence for a few minutes.

I'm considering leaving him out here to go to bed when he asks, 'so why are you on this journey?'

'What do you mean?'

'Realistically, Addy *could* do this alone. Maybe with June to help really sell it to my father but you're a mystery to me. What's in it for you?' I pause before replying, completely taken aback by his huge question. He's basically just implied that I'm disposable.

'We all feel the same about witches, obviously. We found each other in unlikely circumstances and we have to practise in private whilst we watch boys our age get all kinds of apprenticeships. I want that. Why don't we deserve that? I didn't choose to be born a female, so why do boys have this privilege like they're some supreme beings? I deserve a chance, too. We, as women, deserve a chance. I want there to be a change.'

He takes in everything that I'm saying and thinks about it for a moment before answering. I can tell that it's playing on his mind. He looks sad. 'I agree with you. All of the women I've been around in my life have been strong minded, but they were forced to be weak. I don't get to meet many people my age, our age I suppose, and all of the ones I do are people my father wants me to consider marrying. Even those girls, who should be young and full of life, are dull. They've been moulded to fit in. When I'm king, you'll be able to practise wherever you want. You could be the best mage the world has ever seen.'

I look at him, and I don't just mean I look at his pretty face. I *see* him. I see the boy inside a prince. A boy ahead of his time. I see his ideal world, a world in which people are treated as equals. Anyone could love anyone, everyone could do what they were passionate about. I can see equality beaming from his heart. His reign will change *everything*.

'What are you looking at?' he asks, right eyebrow raised again.

'You.'

'Me?'

'Yeah. I can see you.'

'That tends to happen when you look at something.'

'No, I mean I can see *you*. I can see the changes you want to make. I can see your soul and it projects kindness. You're idealistic. You're a true leader. You want to listen to the people and you want to make changes that matter. Like I said, I can see you.'

He blushes. I blink. 'Oh, is the little princeling embarrassed?'

'I'm not embarrassed about *you* thinking that *I'm* an idealistic prince.'

'Then why are you blushing?'

'I'm not.'

'Laurence, I can see the pink filling your cheeks.'

He turns his head away. The prince really *is* blushing and he doesn't want me to know it.

I want to see his face clearly.

I need to see his face clearly.

I cast *pila luminis* and watch as a ball of light grows on my palm, a pale-yellow glow now surrounding us.

'You don't need to see me in any more detail, witch, the moonlight is enough.' He doesn't say *witch* spitefully. He's teasing me, trying to draw out a reaction.

'Well, this is a little bit of moonlight just condensed into my palm.'

'You know the moon doesn't give off light,' he says, pressing his shoulder into mine.

I lay my head on his shoulder as we look at the light dancing across my palm together. It's easy to forget that we've only known each other a few hours.

He closes his hand over mine.

I hate the thought of this moment being over but I whisper the extinguishing spell. '*Exstinguo.*'

The light fades to nothing, but we sit with our heads still resting on each other for a few minutes.

'Okay, witch. I'll catch you in the morning.' He stands and takes my hand to help me up. 'Sleep tight.' His voice is low and breathy as he plants a soft peck my cheek. *He still hasn't let go of my hand.* I turn to walk in the other direction, towards my tent, and he keeps our hands linked until I have to let go to move any further without dragging him with me. I glance over my shoulder and he winks at me again before climbing up the step into the carriage with Charles.

I try to get into our tent without making too much noise, but the prince has taken me by surprise, and I'm fumbling around everywhere. Flo lifts her head to look at me as I trip over her legs. *She's so tall that they reach the end of our tent.*

'What's going on with you?' she asks, dropping her head back down.

'I'll explain in the morning.'

I rest my head on my arm and curl up to sleep, but my brain isn't tired.

My body, however, is exhausted.

I ache from both sleeping on the floor and walking for miles carrying a massive bag.

All I can do is think.

I think about our mission, I think about the journey ahead, I think about the future of our kingdom.

I also think about Laurence.

CHAPTER TWENTY-SEVEN
Addy

It's raining when I wake up on the third morning of our travels. The raindrops are hitting our tent ferociously and I just lay there, listening to the overwhelming sound. I want to get up and start breakfast, I do, but there's no point leaving the tent in this weather. It's also still fairly dark outside so I assume that it's early, even for a cold November morning.

I place my arm over Ottie and snuggle into her. She must have briefly woken up because I feel her wiggle against me. She places one hand over mine and squeezes gently. It's only there for a moment before she's asleep again, and her hand drops back in front of her. I take a deep breath in as she rolls over and I'm greeted with a nose full of her hair. I scrunch my face in a bid not to sneeze but it doesn't work.

It has so much force that my entire body jerks forward.

Ottie jumps out of her sleeping state and almost smacks me in the face when she throws her arms around in a poor attempt at defence. 'Oh, it was you,' she sighs. 'I'm going back to sleep.' She drops her head down onto her right arm and her breathing levels out to a shallow snore within a couple of minutes. *Maybe I should try and get more sleep too? We have quite the walk ahead of us.*

I don't remember falling asleep again but the next thing I know the sun is up and the rain has eased off significantly. The tent is unusually empty because Ottie has already taken herself outside. *Nice of her to wake me up.*

Her, Flo and June are already up, preparing breakfast. Flo is heating the pan whilst June is scrambling eggs and Ottie is slicing bread. *Scrambled eggs on toast for breakfast then.* I'm just settling down on a log close to the already hot fire when Laurence jumps from the carriage with his hands full. In one hand he has a huge bag of sausages, and in the other, some already ground salt and pepper.

'Good morning, Adelaide. I hope you slept well.'

'Morning, Laurence. I slept right through the night on the hard ground. How about you?'

'I almost suffocated Charles because he was

snoring so loudly in the early hours of the morning.'

'Maybe you should have. More food for us this morning,' I joke.

'I *can* hear you,' Charles calls. We all laugh quietly, a joke amongst ourselves.

'Are you not joining us?' I shout back.

'I'll be with you all momentarily.'

'He's changing his underpants,' Laurence whispers. One of his golden eyes shuts quickly whilst the other remains open, looking at me. *He winks a lot for someone who's meant to be proper.*

Laurence strides over to where June is sorting the eggs and hands her the salt and pepper before moving on to Flo with the sausages.

'Don't forget to prick them,' he teases.

Charles clambers out of the carriage with a bale of hay and some water, and wanders over to Larry who is, from what I know about animals, the most well-behaved horse ever. I didn't even hear him stir in the night. Larry snatches the hay out of his hand and pulls a chunk free. He doesn't hold back and I think he could have pulled Charles off his feet if he didn't let go fast enough. Charles walks closer and places a bucket of water on the floor in front of Larry whilst he's distracted. He pats the horse before coming over to the fire and sitting gracefully down next to Laurence. Neither man looks as well put together as they did yesterday. I guess a night sleeping 'rough' did neither of them any good.

Imagine if they had to sleep on the floor.

I thought Clydia and Dru were still asleep but I hear a twig snap behind me and they both appear with a menacing look. 'What have you done?' I ask, eyeing both of the girls as they approach.

'We have treats.' Clydia presents a basket full of bottles filled with orange liquid. 'Freshly squeezed this morning.'

Dru just stands next to her looking proud.

'Heck yeah!' I exclaim, grabbing one out of the basket and popping the lid.

We eat breakfast and chat about our plans for when we arrive in Fairpoint. We talk about whether there's anything we want to do, any sights we want to see. Laurence suggests we take a tour of the old palace grounds and I bounce the idea around for a moment. Before our time, before my parent's time even, the old king lived in a palace that featured part of the Witchbank river. They used to hold witch trials on the grounds for high profile cases. *It seems pretty interesting.*

I've just opened my mouth to take the last bite of egg, pondering my thoughts, when the heavens open and water pours down.

'Everyone in the carriage!' Laurence shouts. The rain is like tiny bits of ice slicing my skin. We run for it. I've never seen the girls move so quickly. Even Charles doesn't complain about us all being in here.

There's a loud clap of thunder and I scream out in surprise.

Everyone laughs and I feel my cheeks flare red with embarrassment, but Dru places her hand on my leg in comfort and I start to relax again. She smiles at me as the carriage lights up with the strike of lightning.

'I'm going to check on Larry. If I'm not back in five minutes then I'm definitely dead. Stay here and stay safe.'

'Sire, let me go.'

'No, you've already done so much for him this morning.'

As soon as he opens the door, rain flies in and he sucks the cold air through his teeth. He braves the elements and I can hear his heavy footsteps as he runs to get to the shelter I made for Larry. The carriage door slams shut as Charles pulls it towards us and the sound of heavy rain is dull against the roof once more. There's three further claps of thunder, and three strikes of lightning between those, before Charles declares that he's going to fetch the prince. None of us make any move to argue as he braces himself for the ice-cold rain again. The pair return a couple of minutes later, completely soaked through but with the assurance that Larry hasn't been spooked and is, in fact, perfectly content in the temporary shelter.

I feel bad that they can't change their wet

clothes with us in the carriage, but I would rather be in here than out there.

The storm continues until early afternoon so we can't start our journey as expected. I had started losing hope at making any progress today when Laurence pipes up.

'Would you like to travel with us?' he asks. We look to June for an answer since she's the one with the plans.

'Well, we *have* now lost a full day of travel because of the storm and the kidnapping.'

'Kidnapping?' he asks, concern plastered across his face.

'We'll explain on the way.'

'Okay, you six pack up your things and we'll ready Larry for the journey.' Charles seems less than enthusiastic about us joining the pair, but he sits up front with Larry so he'll barely know we're here.

It takes us less than ten minutes to pack everything up and begin our travels.

The carriage is slightly too small for all seven of us and our stuff, but we're not uncomfortable, or I'm not, at least.

CHAPTER TWENTY-EIGHT

Adelaide

It feels so good to see the trees passing by. What would have taken us a whole day to walk is now only going to take a couple of hours.

Time is passing quickly and I'm anxiously awaiting our arrival to the capital.

Suddenly there's a *thunk* and the carriage feels like it's ready to tip. We bump together as the carriage jolts to the side and Charles pulls to a stop. I hear him jump down from the front. The sound of his landing is closely followed by a loud sigh.

'I better go and check on the hold-up,' Laurence says, pulling a curtain back to peer outside. *The rain has stopped so at least that's one less thing to worry about.*

'I'll come with you,' I offer. 'I might be able to fix whatever has gone wrong.'

'Okay, let's go.'

The wood creeks as I climb out of the carriage, and it's even louder as Laurence follows me out. 'What's going on?' he asks Charles gently.

'The wheel has split, sire. Probably from too much weight in the carriage.'

'Maybe. The wheels are pretty old though. I was going to replace them before this trip but I forgot to ask.'

'Whatever you say, your highness.'

'I can fix it and reinforce it to hold more weight,' I say. *Bickering isn't going to get us anywhere.* 'Charles, could you possibly fetch some wood to reinforce the spines? It'll need to be dry so you may have to use magic.'

'Oh, I'm not a wizard.'

'Well, Laurence can go instead. You can stay here with me and help repair the split.' He looks completely shocked at my attitude but soon gets his act together as the prince scampers off into the trees.

'As you wish.'

'Do you have anything we can remove this with?' I gesture to the broken wheel.

'We don't. I'm very sorry, young lady.'

'It's okay. We'll just have to do this the hard way.'

I stand back and assess the damage. It looks like

a couple of the spines have snapped and are causing the wheel to struggle. *This is going to be easier if I use magic to bind the wood back together since I can't take the wheel off.*

'Charles, turn around.'

'Why? What's happening?' He spins to face behind him before turning back to me.

'I just don't want you to be incriminated.'

'Not to worry about that, Miss, the number of things I have seen the prince do that he shouldn't. It's my job to help. If the prince isn't worried about you then I'm not either.'

'If you're sure?'

'Just fix it.'

I hold the wheel in my mind as I form the words on my tongue. *'Corruerant instaurabo opus.'*

As soon as I'm through with the incantation, I can see the bonds starting to knit themselves back together. They'll be slightly weaker than the others but strong enough not to break for a second time. I just need Laurence to hurry back with the reinforcement wood so we can get on our way.

I step back to admire my work, and as if by magic, the prince drops a pile of dried wood next to my feet. It's good wood. Thick, strong and most importantly, dry.

'Good job. This all looks great,' I say to him.

'Same to you with the wheel. You've done this before.' He doesn't ask it like a question, it's almost as if he's telling me. Almost as if he knows.

'Oh, just a couple of times. Now, go and hold that wood steady. I'll try not to bind you to the wheel.'

'For a scientist, you don't make me feel very confident about your magic.'

'Just trust me.'

'I've known you less than two days. I can't say I trust you all that much yet. You could be using all of this as a distraction to kill me.'

'Believe me when I say that if we wanted you dead, Clydia would be very upset if we didn't let her do it.'

'Strangely enough. I believe that.'

I reinforce every spine on the wheel with a second piece of wood *without* accidentally binding the prince to the carriage. Laurence wiggles the wheel and looks up at me, obviously content.

'Seems secure. Ready to roll?'

I nod. 'Let's hope it doesn't break again.'

Charles is already back up front when I climb up the step and back into the carriage. I'm greeted with a chorus of questions about what happened and I have to give my brain half a second to process any of them. 'The wheel fractured but don't worry, I've repaired and reinforced it. We'll just have to take it a bit slower so it doesn't break again.'

I didn't realise that the prince had climbed up behind me until I hear his voice over my shoulder.

'She fixed it and didn't stick me to the wheel. What a delightful time.'

'I do my best.'

'I can tell.' He offers me a wink before turning to the rest of the girls. 'Now, let's get back to it ladies, or we won't be in the capital for another week.'

Charles teases Larry's reigns and we're moving again, but with a bit more care this time. 'As much as I love seeing your beautiful faces,' Laurence says, 'I think it might be worth glamouring yourselves. Preferably as men. The city will tear me apart if they catch wind of the fact I'm in a carriage on my way back to the city with an group of women.'

'They also wouldn't take us seriously.'

'You're right there.'

We each take it in turns to change into different versions of ourselves. We get taller, our faces harsher, our shoulders broader and our hair shorter. It's a lot more cramped in here with our new appearances. The prince also changes back into the grizzly man he was when we first met.

We're a different group of people in the carriage now. A group of people you definitely wouldn't want to approach.

'What do your parents think of you all doing this? I'm assuming they don't know the real reason you're visiting the capital.' The entire carriage tenses.

I kind of speak for more than just two of us in

this situation. 'None of us have parents. They're either dead or disowned us when they discovered we were witches. We're the only family each other has. We are just one family of unlikely friends that became close enough to trust each other.'

The prince is silent for a moment before he manages to stutter a few words. 'I...I'm sorry. I feel positively awful for asking. Please, accept my apologies.'

'You weren't to know,' Dru replies.

'So, you've done this all on your own? The six of you?'

'Yes,' I answer, not meaning to be blunt but also wanting to plainly state the facts. 'I know what you're thinking though. We've got big dreams for such little girls.'

'I actually think the six of you are some of the most inspirational people I've ever met. I've never had to experience anything like this. Not having your real families is bad enough but to be shunned for what should be a basic human right, for you to practise, is completely unfair. I've seen the magic you can do. You're just as good as any young wizard I've met and you haven't had any professional training. You could be some our greatest assets if we gave you the chance.'

I can feel June riling herself up to reprimand the prince before she fires herself at him.

'One: we're not just *shunned*. We're murdered.

There are witch trials going on up and down the country as we speak, which are being completed by wizards. Men are threatened by women being their equals because they don't think they'll be able to hold the power. That's not what we want. We just want equal opportunities. Why is that so much to ask for? Two: we *are* each other's real family. In fact, these girls have been more my family than anyone else in my life. They support me, they care for and about me, they make sure I'm safe and they always, *always* consider how I'm feeling. I hope they feel the same way about how I treat them too.' There's a succession of nods from all of us. 'All of that from a group of people who didn't know each other a few years ago. I think that's extraordinary.'

She went easy on him. I'm impressed. I thought she would go in all guns blazing since he's a *royal*. Someone who can actually bring change. I suppose if she did that, though, we would just look crazy. Her speech for the king is just as tame, but we've been working on that for months. This came from her heart. The place where her burning passions for the things she believes in meet.

'I didn't realise how unfair it was until I was older. I grew up blinded by the idea that women shouldn't be allowed to practise magic because they would be too dangerous. I don't have a sister to consider and I don't remember much of my mother. She died when Thomas was born. She was gentle yet strong, that's what I've always told myself. I know Aeron remembers more but he would never tell me. I can only apologise on behalf of the court and I promise you with my whole heart, I promise you with the risk of my reign, that I will do everything in my power to get you an audience with my father as soon as I possibly can. This has to change.' His eyes are harsh as he speaks.

Determined.

'It's our mission to get the kingdom to see us in a different light. Addy created this shield, this entire wall of defence for the army. She did it with her female brain and it's her female magic that's currently sitting in the core. We deserve a chance.'

I can see pride beaming off Ottie as she throws her arms around me, almost smacking the prince square in the nose. If he hadn't backed out of the way in time, I think she might have. 'I'm so proud of you. You're intelligent, passionate and strong. Mum and Dad would be so proud of you for fighting for something we both believe in so strongly. I can feel them in my heart, pushing all of this love and pride your way.' I twist the bracelet June gave us just a few days ago between my fingers.

Tears fall down my cheeks as I hug her back. To everyone else we look like two grown men embracing each other in a hug, a hug that's in no way attempting to be masculine, but I can feel Ottie underneath. This is my sister and she's maturing into a strong, confident woman. I couldn't be prouder. I clear my throat as I loosen myself from her grip.

'Well, let's get back to our mission. The battle of fairness versus injustice hasn't been won yet.'

CHAPTER TWENTY-NINE
Clydia

It's starting to get dark when Laurence bangs on the roof of the carriage, signalling to Charles that he wants to stop. He climbs out and I hear him ask Charles to find a safe place to set up camp tonight. I strain my ears a little more and hear Charles offer to continue on to the next town. 'We need the progress and we can find an inn there. It'll be much more comfortable than spending another night in this carriage.'

'A night under the stars is good for the soul, Charles. I'm also kind of enjoying spending time with these girls. They're interesting.'

'Interesting, sire?'

'Yes, Charles. Interesting. Like I find them pleasant and actually quite entertaining to be around.'

'As you wish. Although, they could stay at the inn too.'

No other words are exchanged but there's still a couple of moments before Laurence appears back in the carriage. He briefs us on the plan and Addy has to remind him that our tents are still wet from last night.

'You can stay in here, with Charles and I. There's plenty of space.'

'Plenty of space?' June starts. 'There's barely enough space for the seven of us to sit in here, let alone lay down comfortably and have Charles in here too.'

'I'll dry them off when we stop, then.' I want to hit him for being so annoying, but I decide against the idea when I remember that he's the future king so someone I really don't want to make an enemy of.

A few minutes later the carriage slows and we all climb out. Charles has pulled up on the side of the track and asks if we can make our own way to a clearing since he probably won't be able to get the carriage down there.

'Fine, fine, have it your way,' Laurence starts. 'We'll go and find somewhere to stay in the next town but we need to get there quickly. You know Larry doesn't like to work in the dark.' Laurence pushes Charles to respond but instead he climbs back onto the front and takes Larry's reigns in his hands.

Relief washes over me as we all squash back

into the carriage. A night of not sleeping on the floor sounds like a dream right now, and if we're with the prince then the inn will be a nice one. Probably one with a bar for us to celebrate in. One last hurrah before the real work starts and we each put our lives in more danger.

Dusk has set in when we arrive in the town. There isn't a sign in sight that tells us the name of where we are. It's most peculiar.

The inn does look beautiful though. It's an old building that's been well maintained over the years. Someone cares about this little inn and it really shows.

The face of the woman on the reception desk is a sight to see when eight men pile through the door and stand in front of her asking for rooms.

'Sorry for the look of surprise. We don't usually get many people around these parts.' Her voice is soft and she's mastered the shocked look that once sat across her face.

'Not to worry, Miss. Please can we have enough rooms to sleep eight?' Laurence asks. He's softened his grizzly voice too, in a bid to not scare the young lady.

'Yes, of course. How many nights?'

'Just the one. Oh, and do you have space for our horse and carriage?'

'We have a barn out the back which is nearly always empty. You can bring it round there. I'll make sure they're both well cared for.'

She hands over four keys for adjoining rooms on the first floor. Charles follows her outside to bring Larry and the carriage to the barn whilst we pile our way up the first flight of stairs.

It looks like we're the only guests tonight.

We partner up in our usual sleeping arrangements and each pair takes a key. June and I head for the room closest to the stairs. I like knowing I can jump up and kill any intruders before the other girls can even swing their legs out of bed. Addy and Ottie take the room next to us with Flo and Dru behind them.

We give Laurence and Charles the back room so they're out of harm's way.

If anything were to happen, there would be a whole line of defence before it reached them.

I would be the first one up and ready to attack. I always sleep with my knife strapped to my calf.

Charles is back before we've even closed our doors. He approves of us pressuring Laurence into the back room, which I think gets us some extra credit with him. With his dismissal, I head to mine and June's room. All I want to do is clean my hair and body. This inn has hot running water that falls into a deep bath. The soap smells of lavender and there's even separate shampoo and conditioner. This is a luxury I have never experienced but let me tell you, I want to. I close the door to our room, trapping

June and I inside.

'I'm going for a bath.'

'Okay. I'll have one after you. I'm going to unpack my bag and see if anything needs drying off. Want me to do yours too?'

'You would be an absolute gem if you did.'

'I gotcha.' She shoots finger guns my way and I roll my eyes as I move to draw a bath. She's like an embarrassing old man sometimes, but I love her for it.

I collapse into the hot, soapy water and my muscles relax into the heat. They're grateful for the sweet relief. I didn't realise how much I ached until I stopped moving. I start to reflect on our journey so far but I decide against it. It's in the past and all I can do is focus on the here and now, or the future. There's no use looking back. I never want to live that life again. In that life, I never would have stayed in an inn as nice as this one.

What is it the girl at the front desk had said?

They don't get many visitors in this area?

I want to ask her about that.

I hold my breath and let my head fall beneath the water. It feels good to untangle the braids that keep my hair held in place at all times. The loose strands curl around my head as I run my fingers over my scalp. When I can't hold my breath any longer, I sit up and let the water run off of me. The inn has given us two wash cloths so I grab the one closest to me, saturate it with water, pick up the floral smelling soap and rub it on the cloth. I want to viciously scrub my body but instead I gently move the cloth in slow circles. It isn't that I'm really dirty, but after three days travelling with no shower, I'm not exactly clean.

Once I've rinsed the soap off, I lay my head far enough in the water to cover my hair and hold it there until it makes my neck ache. I reach out for the shampoo and lather the small blob in my hands. I massage the sweet smell into the roots of my hair before collecting the length onto my head and savagely scrunching the shampoo through. Satisfied that I'm fully covered, I lay back down in the water and rinse the bubbles out.

I remember washing my hair in the institute with cheap soap that didn't smell of anything. I was barely allowed to dry my body before I was rushed back to my room to dress.

Today I'm going to take my time running the conditioner through my thick, black curls.

I wonder who I got my curls from? I wish I could remember something about my parents, anything at all, but when I try to think of them my mind just draws blank. Were they funny? Did they love each other? All I know for sure is that both of them had dark skin - mine a reflection of their own. The thing that confuses me the most is that my ice blue eyes are a stark contrast to my skin and hair. Is it another sign of being a witch or is it just sheer coincidence? Did my parents have eyes like this too? There are so many questions that I just wish someone could answer.

I leave the conditioner in another couple of minutes. More and more questions about my life before the institute fly through my mind. The only family I consider myself to have were strangers to me at different times of my life. I've never had anyone there from the beginning like some of the girls.

I'm still in my own head when June calls through. 'Are you almost done in there? My body is dying to be cleaned.'

'Yeah, I'll be out in a sec.'

I quickly wash the conditioner from my hair and squeeze out the excess water. I pull the plug and hop out of the bath, flipping my hair forward and pulling a towel over it. I rub the long strands between the fabric to dry it off a little. We only have two towels in here so I wrap the damp one around my body and leave the other neatly folded for June.

'It's all yours' I tell her.

'You took your time.'

'When you've got hair like this, everything takes longer.'

***

'You know earlier you said that you don't many visitors around here?'

'Yeah...' The woman on the desk looks worried. Her voice remains gentle though.

'What did you mean by that?'

'This town is notorious for witch trials. An extraordinary number of women have drowned in the depths of Colend lake. It's actually been renamed Witches End. Those that didn't drown were hung on that permanently raised platform in the middle of town. You'll see it if you head out to the tavern tonight. They've basically put it on a stage for all to see.'

'Who do you mean when you say 'they'?'

She twists a strand of her shoulder length brown hair while she answers me. 'The witch hunters, of course. We had the most witch hunters in the kingdom at one point. It was too overwhelming to even go outside. I don't suppose that you're one, are you?'

'A witch?'

'A witch hunter. You have to be a woman to be a witch.'

I forgot about the glamour I'd reinstated before I left the room. 'I'm not a witch hunter, no. Are you?'

'No.'

'Then I'm glad that's settled.' I turn to walk away but she grabs my arm. I pull away in shock.

'What's your name?' she asks. Her blue eyes

shine out of her pale skin. She's staring at me, making it more obvious that she's trying to see past my glamour.

'Clyde. Yours?'

'River.'

'See you around, River.' I slip out of the door to explore the town before the others notice I'm gone.

CHAPTER THIRTY
Clydia

Laurence is with Larry when I try to sneak back in. I've only been gone around half an hour but there really is nothing to do here.

'Where have you been?' I hear the words from behind me. I thought I had managed to creep past him but I guess he's used to listening out for anyone he isn't expecting.

'I've been around. Why are you out here?'

'Sometimes I like to just spend some time with Larry. His life is devoted to taking me where I need to go. I think he deserves some sugar cubes and nose pats for that.'

'You're right.' I take a sugar cube from next to where he's sitting and hold it flat in my hand. Larry takes it gently and nudges his nose against me in approval. I stroke my hand along his white fur and give him a quick scratch under the chin.

'Ha, he likes you. Who would have thought?'

'I would have thought. I'm a charming individual.'

'Who could kill me in her sleep.'

'Technicalities. You're a prince that gives his horse a name that's a shortened version of his own.'

'It makes it feel like he's part of me.'

'Whatever you say, princeling.'

Larry nudges me for another sugar cube and I'm all too happy to oblige. I spend some time out here with him and Laurence, just to be away from the others for a while.

'You know, if this goes well for you, I could use a new bodyguard? It wouldn't be too strenuous. It's just Charles is getting a bit older and can't wield a sword the way he used to. It also means you could use some of that magic you have simmering underneath your skin.'

The offer takes me by surprise. We've known the prince a matter of days and he already trusts me to protect his life. He must be out of his mind.

'You're joking?'

'Not at all. For some ungodly reason, I feel safe around you. Maybe it's because murdering me would be high treason, but you know, could be any other reason too.'

'I have a family, Laurence. The girls.'

'I don't need an answer right now. Take your time. Please, just make sure you survive your encounter with my father.'

'That's the plan.'

We take the back entrance inside. It's so narrow, we have to climb the stairs single file. Every step we take makes the building creak. We reach the first floor and head to our rooms. He grabs my arm to stop me just before I open my door. *What is it with people doing that today?*

'Yes?' I ask.

He looks embarrassed. His voice is a whisper compared to his usual authority. 'Can you please take care of Drusilla? I'm quite fond of her and I would never be able to forgive myself if something happened to her. Especially by my father's hand.'

'You have my word.'

I turn the brass handle and swing the door open. June is sitting on the bed in a towel still, picking through her dry clothes to find some nightwear.

'I thought you had gone off wondering,' she scolds, 'until I saw you out of the window feeding the horse sugar cubes with Laurence. You should have told me where you were going. I was worried sick when I came through and you weren't in the room.'

'Sorry, Mum,' I tease. She doesn't look impressed. 'I can look after myself out there. Don't you worry.'

'You were meant to be looking after Ottie too and look where that got us.'

'That's different.'

'Is it?'

I feel a pang of guilt for what happened to Ottie. *Was it my fault?* Maybe June is right and I should go and apologise to her.

I've felt so many things today that I don't usually feel. How do I even begin?

***

We all make our way out the back to sit with Larry. It's nice to be outside, and after the story of the witch hunters, I'm not fancying my chances of being out in the open again. Even if we are all glamoured.

'Hey, Clydia?' My heart squeezes whenever she speaks. All I can remember is my promise to Laurence. I brush it off and remember who I am. What I can do.

'What's up my little Dru bear?'

'One: stop that. Two: if you guys fancy going for a hunt then I'll cook dinner tonight.'

'The only thing I trust you to cook is pancakes,' June badgers.

'Okay, I'll go and hunt with Clydia then.'

'You'll definitely fall and hurt yourself,' Flo jokes, nudging her shoulder playfully.

I'm so into bickering with the girls that I forgot Laurence is here until he speaks.

'How about we find something to eat in a

tavern. I'm sure there's one around here.'

'Did you not hear what I said about the witch hunters?'

'We're glamoured,' he speaks as if being caught won't get us killed.

'Well, I'm not here to risk it again. Being bound and kicked is, surprisingly, no fun at all,' Ottie adds.

'I'll bring it back then. I'm sure they'll have some kind of takeaway.'

'It's your funeral.'

***

Less than an hour later, Laurence comes swanning in with an old apple crate covered in gingham cloth. 'Dinner is served.' He whips the cloth off and it's full of perfectly golden pies. 'We have chicken and mushroom here,' he points to the biggest one. *Clearly his favourite then.* 'Cheese and onion here,' he has to lift the chicken and mushroom one out to show us. It's squashed down in the corner with a broken crust and filling spilling out. 'Finally, we have dessert.' He gently lifts out the final pie and places it on the collection of wooden barrels that we've fashioned into a table. 'Apple and blackberry. The champion of all sweet pies.'

'That's a lot of pie,' Dru notes whilst her eyes are hungrily scanning every single one of them.

'It's all they had, princess.'

'I'm sure they'd serve me better in your palace. Also, don't you dare call me princess again. I'm the queen of this kingdom.'

'If only you could tell that to my mother.'

There's an awkward silence. It's common knowledge not to speak about the queen around the royal family. Her death was a shock to the entire kingdom. We mourned for weeks at her passing. The kind queen, the queen that loved to give back, the queen that kept the king sane. The king basically outlawed every word spoken about her. Nobody dared use her name around a member of the royal family, but Laurence laughed it off like it was nothing.

'The look on all your faces,' he's almost crying with laughter. 'You *can* speak of her around me. I remember her fondly. I can't say the same for my father and Aeron though.'

Dru thumps him right in the arm.

'What was that for?'

'Making us all worry that we were about to commit a high offence. You deserve a thump for that.'

'Just eat your damn pie. I risked my life for this delicious food and you're not being very grateful.'

'Oh, thank you, kind prince, future king of the Delgosi Isles,' she mocks. 'Thank you for risking your life out there in those hordes of witch hunters to fetch us these baked goods. We would have gone hungry if it weren't for you.'

The look on his face does not reflect light humour. I think he's ready to thump Dru back. I would. He looks her dead in the eye as he picks up a forkful of chicken and mushroom pie. 'Mmmm delicious.'

The weather has started to turn bitter and the tense atmosphere makes it even worse. I bundle further into the barn and ask Laurence about the palace security.

'It's my job to keep everyone safe and I can only do that if I know what to expect when I'm there. I'll scope it out when we arrive but maybe you can give me an idea of what to look out for and when.'

'What do you think is going to be happening? It's not a heist. You're just trying to get an audience.'

'Well...' I pause. Was this a wise thing to tell the prince? Maybe the threat would make him less likely to help us or maybe it would make him beg for us to have an audience. He said he wanted to help.

'Well?'

'Well, if we don't get an audience then we'll have to force our way inside. The only way to force ourselves inside is to know the security measures.'

Charles has been silent for most of the night, only speaking when spoken to, but I watch as both of their faces turned pale. *Good to know that they see me as a threat.*

'At least let them fight fair. Use a sword and duel them. Don't just kill my guards.'

'It'll create too much of a disturbance. I don't want everyone to know my business. I just want to get in and get out. No questions asked.'

'How about you trust that I'm going to be able to get you a formal audience so you don't have to risk both trespassing and murder charges?'

'You ask so much of me, princeling. It's in my blood to hurt anything that poses a danger to me.'

'Clydia, he's right.' It's Addy's time to pipe up. 'Maybe avoid killing any guards while you can? They're only doing their job. They have to keep the king safe. I'm sure more people would care if *he* were killed, than one of us.'

'Speak for yourself,' Dru argues. 'But I do think we should all be trained in combat. I would love to know how to wield a sword.' She jumps around like she's swinging a huge weapon. 'Clydia barely lets any of us touch her knife.'

Laurence wiggles his eyebrows. 'Well you all better get a good night's sleep then because I'll spend tomorrow morning training you out here. It's going to be hard work but at least you'll look like more convincing men. I'll meet you here at sunrise.'

With that, he leaves us, taking Charles with him.

We watch as they take the road that leads into town.

'Where the heck is he going at this time?' Flo

asks, looking after the prince and his hand with furrowed brows.

'You'll be lucky if I know. He's more unpredictable than Dru.'

'Hey!' She pulls on a mask of hurt.

'Don't act insulted.'

'Well if this crazy man wants us to be up and ready to train at the crack of dawn then we better head up to bed.' Flo is usually the sensible one but this time it's June who makes the suggestion.

'You're probably right,' I agree. I stand to make my way up to bed and the others follow. Dru looks back to the path and I think, just for a moment, that she's going to stay in the cold and wait. When the five of us reach the back door, she finally pats Larry on the nose and leaves him to rest for the night.

It isn't until the next morning, when Flo wakes us, that we realise Dru is missing from her bed. She isn't in the bathroom and she isn't outside.

It isn't even light out and already someone else is missing.

We don't bother to check if Laurence and Charles made it back. We all just dress and storm out of the inn.

I may not know where she is but there is one thing I'm certain on.

I'm going to kill her when I find her.

CHAPTER THIRTY-ONE
Clydia

It feels like we've been searching for hours before the sun even rises. Funny how slowly time passes when you're in pursuit of your missing best friend.

'If she's been stupid enough to go into town and get captured then I'm going to kill her.'

'Take it easy, Clydia, she's probably just gone for a wander and is back in bed none the wiser to us being out here.'

'I'm still going to kill her, Flo.'

'Let's just head back. Laurence will be waiting for us and we can use the extra set of eyes. Two if Charles is getting involved.' Ottie has actually come up with a pretty good idea, here. I'm mad that I didn't think of it first, too lost in the mess of my own mind.

'You're right,' I agree. 'Let's go before someone wakes up and realises that we're not glamoured out here.'

We didn't venture far at all, so we're back before the sun has even fully risen. Flo is almost frantic when we arrived back, itching to get back out there and search for the girl she feels most responsible for.

It takes us all a moment to register the familiar red hair whipping around in the breeze.

I'm going to kill her.

She's tied it back into a ponytail for training, but some strands are still hitting her in the face as she speaks to Laurence.

I'm going to kill her.

If only Flo hadn't beat me to it. 'Where the heck have you been? We've been out looking for you since the early hours of this morning. We thought you had been kidnapped!'

'I came downstairs to sit in the library because I couldn't sleep. The library is in no way a library, by the way. There are barely enough books to fill a shelf. A few minutes after I had decided on a book, Laurence came in and we were sat together for a while. I did leave a note. It was on my bed.'

'I didn't see any note.'

'Oh, I'll show you when we go back upstairs. I'm sorry for making you all worry. I just didn't want to wake you up by turning the torch on.' She lowers her head and puts on her best puppy dog eyes.

'Did you not wonder where I was when you came back to the room to change?'

'The sun had already started to rise so I just assumed you were outside waiting for us. We haven't been out here long. Maybe a minute or two.'

Flo grabs her into a hug before I can reach her and wallop her round the head, but I guess I can wait until later. Honestly, I'm more intrigued about what her and Laurence were talking about for hours.

'Everyone ready to get started?' Laurence asks, breaking up the conversation. I look down at the pile of swords next to his feet and my heart starts to sing.

'Oh, we're ready.'

'Clydia, I knew you would be ready. I'm more asking the others.'

'Well, don't direct the question to all of us then.'

'Fine. Ottie, Addy, Flo, June, and Dru... are you ready? Are you ready to become as ruthless as Clydia? Are you ready to be able to hold a sword and know what you're going to do with it?'

'I think so,' Ottie replies.

'Honestly, I'd rather not wield a blade at another human. I don't want to hurt anyone.'

'You don't have to use these skills, Addy, but it'll be good for us all to have them. Just in case...'

She nods, although not with confidence. 'Okay.'

Ottie always knows what to say when it comes to convincing Addy to do something outside of her comfort zone. Sometimes I wish I weren't so willing to try everything. I think it makes me look like I have no remorse for my actions. I do, I just like to be prepared for every situation. Better to know how to fight than die in an already lost battle.

I glance over at Flo and June who nod in unison. They're both ready for the action to start too. Laurence sees the gesture and draws his weapon.

'Right then ladies. Put one of these on,' he points us to a pile of heavy chainmail vests, 'and choose your sword. Practice is about to begin.'

***

Laurence taught us the basics of how to handle a sword so 'we don't injure ourselves'. *He's a surprisingly good tutor for a princeling.* Now we're moving on to using the sword in combat. Excitement is coursing through my veins and I'm ready to learn how a royal wields a weapon. I've only ever used my knife. I find it easier to keep to the one weapon so you can fight with stealth, but now there's another blade in my hand and I'm starting to regret not learning how to use it sooner.

The sword is heavy, and it hurts to hold up for too long. I'm strong but these swords definitely weren't built for my body shape. I need something light and nimble. Something easy to swing around with a blade longer than my dagger, but lighter than this thing.

'I've known you a matter of days and I already don't trust you to practice with each other, so I have these.' He ducks into the barn and carries out human shaped bales of hay one by one.

'Is this guy joking?' Ottie asks. 'He wants us to stick a sword in Larry's food?'

'Looks like it,' Addy replies. He drags one out and places it in front of her.

'Do you have a better idea, Marie Curie?'

'I would love to work for a woman as intelligent as Marie Curie so thanks for the comparison, Laurence.'

'It was sarcasm but okay. Although, I reckon one day I could see you working with her team. You have the smarts. You'll have to travel across kingdoms to do it but I'm sure we can arrange something.'

I can tell that she wants to believe him.

She holds up her sword, ready to strike the dummy. 'Are we doing this?' Deflecting the attention. Classic Addy.

By the time we've finished practise the ground is covered in loose hay. Larry would be in his element if Laurence let him out. He shut Larry away as soon as we picked up the swords in fear of us injuring him. Smart really.

'Right, I think you all have the basics. You can keep the swords but please sheath them if you're not in combat. You'll end up killing each other if not. It's your choice if you include them in your glamour, but from experience I would. It will deter others from trying anything.'

'You have way too much trust in these losers,' I joke. 'There's a reason I don't let them near my dagger.'

'Honestly, I'm more worried about you. *You're ruthless*. I just hope I don't die by the hand of my own soldier.'

'I'm not your soldier and you should continue to not test my patience. Just so we don't have any issues.'

'On that note, we need to start getting ready to leave. We spent longer than I expected out here and Charles is giving me absolute death stares from our window.' We turn to face the prince's window and Charles isn't looking impressed. The sun is already high in the sky and I can tell that he just wants to get back to palace life.

For a morning in mid-November it's surprisingly warm. We're all drenched in sweat and I'm sure we stink. I turn back and see that Laurence has barely shed a single bead of water from his pores. He's worked as hard as the rest of us. Constantly standing with us to show the correct stance, training next to us so we could reference his technique. He's done all of it, yet he's barely shed a glimmer of sweat.

I realise now that he's worked hard to be as

skilled as he is. I really respect that.

It's the middle of the afternoon before we're on the road, but the prince decides that we should travel through the night. Larry is well rested, and Laurence can create a ball of light for Charles that will last more than a few hours. We're finally on our way to the capital and it feels good. If there's no disruptions to our journey now, then we'll be there a day early. Perfect time for me to assess security and explore the city.

The darkness draws in quickly and most of the girls have fallen asleep to the gentle lull of the carriage. I've just started to close my eyes when I tune in on some whispers.

'You did really well out there today. I thought you would make a joke out of it, but you really stepped up.' The voice is low. *Laurence.*

'Thanks. I can't help but think that if we knew how to fight, nobody would have died.' *Is that Dru feeling guilty about something she didn't do?*

'What do you mean?'

'I know that Jake, Felix and the other guy would have used magic anyway, but my brain keeps telling me that a physical fight would have been fairer.'

'They would have killed you, Dru. I really am thankful that Flo is a witch with a strong maternal instinct because it means that you're still alive.'

'You wouldn't have known any other way if I

wasn't.'

'And what a sad world that would have been.'

I open my eyes just a little and I can just about see that Dru is leaning into Laurence. His arm is draped around her shoulders with her head gently on his shoulder.

'Did you come up with a mission name for this morning?' His voice whispers into her hair. Her eyes have closed, and she's taking comfort in him being intimate with her.

'Not everything needs a mission name.' Her voice is barely a whisper. I can tell that she's falling asleep because the Dru I know would have jumped at giving something a mission name. There's silence for a few moments, only broken by the sound of Larry's hooves trotting along and the rattle of stones as our carriage passes over a few loose ones.

'Operation: Steel,' her voice is even quieter than before. Barely audible over the hooves clip-clopping.

'I like it. It sounds dangerous but strong. A bit like you.' She doesn't reply. He gives her a little nudge and when she still doesn't answer, a quick kiss on the head. Taking in the smell of her hair.

I close my eyes quickly. I've already stolen enough of their moment. The prince isn't my type, I'd rather he was a princess if I'm honest, but I know Dru will find comfort in him and I'm happy for her. In the morning they won't be snuggling like this and neither of them will speak a word of the stolen moments shared.

They're both asleep before me.

I hear Laurence's gentle snores and I want to throw something at him, but I can just make out his figure, and he's still holding Dru close. Even in his sleep, he wants someone to protect her. I should tell him that she's strong enough to look after herself. She has been all the years I've known her, and she will in the future, too.

His snoring stops and he opens his eyes slowly. He must have caught me looking at him because he smiles as he moves Dru off him and leans her carefully against the side of the carriage. He offers me a silent salute using his middle and index fingers, the salute of a soldier, before closing his eyes and quickly drifting back off to sleep.

I have a lot to think about when it comes to Laurence and his offer, but I can't focus on that right now. I need to rest, to prepare, for when the sun rises and tomorrow comes. We're getting closer and closer to our fates and I'm more scared of dying than I will ever let on.

Flo is leaning against me with her head resting on my shoulder. There's something special about having a connection with someone you really care about. Flo and I share a unique trust. A trust that we will both do whatever it takes to keep the others safe. No questions asked. I place my head gently on hers, knowing that she'll keep me safe, too.

Now the seventh sacrifice to the gentle rocking of the carriage, my body falls victim to the land of nod.

CHAPTER THIRTY-TWO
June

It's taking longer than expected to arrive. Charles said we stopped a few times during the night for Larry to drink and rest, but it's already pushing into late afternoon by the time I wake. Some of the others are still asleep. The only people awake are me, Laurence, Flo and Addy. I try to stretch my body out without hitting anyone in the face, but I feel the tips of my fingers tickle Dru's cheeks. She makes an agitated noise and scratches at her face. She doesn't wake up, though. She's the last one asleep, in fact, she sleeps until we arrive at the outskirts of Fairpoint.

'Morning sunshine,' Clydia chimes. 'Just in time to see our entrance to the big city.'

'We're here already?' Dru is groggy and I can already tell that her neck will be stiff from the angle of her head.

'Yeah. You've been asleep for hours. The sun

will be setting by the time we reach the centre.'

I knew the capital was big, but we pass housing clusters that are basically the size of Eastfall with their own markets at the centre. They pave the way to the middle of the city which circles around the new palace at the centre.

'This is insane.' I'm completely in awe. There's something beautiful about dusk in any landscape, but when the sun is setting behind a palace with a glass ceiling... its breath taking.

'Welcome to my home. She's beautiful, isn't she?'

I peel my eyes away from the scene to glance at Laurence. He seems as awestruck as the rest of us. I bet this view will never get old.

I wish I could capture this moment and keep it safe forever.

He places his hand on Dru's back and I suddenly feel like I'm in a moment that shouldn't involve me. I can see what's happening between them, but it isn't my place to ask. I want her to trust me enough to tell me if there's anything going on. I wonder if anyone else has spotted their secret touches and quick glances?

'There's an inn just around the corner from the palace. I'll ask Charles to get a couple of rooms set up for you. Don't glamour yourselves in there because the innkeeper can see right through them. Just act like yourselves but *do not* show any sign of being witches.'

'Just a light warning then.' Ottie is really growing into a second Clydia, who I can sense is proud of her for the sarcastic comment.

'Do you want to die by witch trial?' Stone cold sincerity is plastered across Laurence's face.

'Our plans are basically a suicide mission anyway.' She's so quick to dismiss his threats, clearly in disbelief that anything bad can happen this close to the palace. I think she's forgotten that we're in the capital city. There are enough people to watch for these things. They look for people like us.

Laurence continues his point. 'Your plans *are* for the greater good and it would be a noble way to die if the worst-case scenario did happen. I know you'll make it out though. I'll be in there with you if I can. It's my duty as the future king to know what is happening in the kingdom.'

'I'll hold you to that.'

We hang around close to the carriage until we receive the all clear from Charles. He took his time getting back to us even though it isn't that far of a walk. We're 'just around the corner' after all. He returns just as darkness engulfs the sky and the lanterns strung up across streets light the way. I can't help but think, if the lanterns weren't lighting the skies, you could lay in any room on the top floor of the palace and see the stars forming constellations above you.

Don't get me wrong, it will always look magical, but there's something about tonight's sunset that holds a place in my heart already.

'I could only get two rooms but they both have double beds, so you'll have to cram three in each.'

'That's fine. Thank you for arranging this, Charles.' It's almost like Flo takes the words right out of my mouth.

'I agree, thank you so much. Your kindness will not be forgotten.' I have this need to show my gratitude for everything that's done for me, especially out of the goodness of someone's heart.

'It was at the prince's orders, but you are still most welcome. Both rooms are booked under the name, 'Coraline'. They know to expect six of you over the two rooms.'

He prepares Larry to take the carriage back into the palace grounds. 'Best be getting on then. The werewolves and vampires will be out before you know it.' He chuckles to himself as he rides away.

'I just can't figure that man out. Does he want to be friends with us or not?'

'You know what, June, I don't think even he knows.' Ottie is speaking some sense for the first time in days. 'But whether he's our friend or not, we all heard what he said. Let's get going before all the creepies come out for the night.' The child in her is still strong. Of course, she doesn't want to hang about in the dark.

The inn is nice, really nice. Much nicer than any place I've ever stayed, anyway. It's small and hidden, but it makes the other inn look like a barn. It feels like a home away from home more than a temporary place to stay. I just hope we can afford the extra night since we haven't *actually* spent any of the money we brought with us. Laurence is proving to be helpful in more ways than one.

Our rooms are at the back of the top floor, so we're well out of the way. We drop our things into both rooms and then gather together in the one furthest from the stairs. Addy, Ottie and Clydia are sharing this room and Dru, Flo and I are sharing the room next door.

'What's the plan for tomorrow then?' If we have all of our plans sorted out for tomorrow, I can probably make it through the day without having a meltdown.

'I really would like to spend some time at Witchbank river. The history is pretty crazy, and I think paying respect to the women that came before us might put fate on our side.' Flo believes in things like fate and, honestly, I think I'm starting to agree with her views.

'I'm definitely down for that, but *please* can we go after I've assessed how palace security is looking?'

'Sure, we'll go at noon. You can do what you like before then but be safe. All of you.'

'Clydia, I'll come with you,' Ottie offers.

'It would be good to have a second set of eyes. We can go as soon as we wake in the morning. We should have a couple of hours then.'

'Perfect.'

'There's a library near the old palace that I'd like to see.'

'I've heard of that. The Mary Wollstonecraft library right, Flo?'

'Yeah, that's it. Should we head there in the morning?'

'That's us sorted,' Addy replies. 'We'll be near Witchbank river too.'

'I was actually hoping that I would be able to catch Laurence out on his morning ride.' We all turn to face Dru, feigning surprise. 'I know you all know so don't act so shocked.'

'Yeah, you're right. We can all see the sneaky glances at one other. So, tell us, what's going on?' *I really want to know.* None of us have ever spoken about romantic interests, assuming that's what this is.

'He's funny, kind, understands my sense of humour. He makes me feel special without even trying. I find comfort in just being with him. I feel all this after just a few days and I'm still trying to figure out what it means. I think I like him as more than a friend, but I can't focus on that now. I might not get to see him after the mission is over. I could be dead.'

'You can't think like that, Dru. If you're feeling something more then you should speak to him about it. Would you rather die with your truth being told and potentially having a day or so to have some fun, or die having never told him how you're feeling? He's obviously feeling something more too. He's not sneaking touches and glances with any of us.'

'Thanks, June, but I think I would rather not live with the embarrassment of telling him before the mission. I'll be distracted if he rejects me and I can't be distracted.'

'Only you know how you're feeling and only you know what you want. If you want to talk about it more with us, then I'm going to be here to listen. We all are.'

'You're the best.' We gather in a group hug and a sudden wave of hope comes over me.

I never want to let go of this moment. *Ever.*

CHAPTER THIRTY-THREE
June

I decide to tag along with Addy and Flo. This library sounds interesting, it's close to the old palace and it's named after a European advocate for women's rights. It's happening in Europe and it's happening here, with us. Europe isn't part of our world. In fact, our kingdom isn't involved in world events.

It doesn't take long to reach the library. It towers over the old palace remains. One day in the past it could have been a part of the palace, but now it stands alone. It stands tall. It stands above the other buildings in the area and it's simply beautiful.

We head inside and the colours are perfect compliments of each other. Dark oak shelves give way to a white marble floor with a charcoal grey carpet running down the centre aisle. The black ornate stairs spiral up to the next floor and, I'm sure, the many floors after that. The ceilings are high, supported by wooden beams that match the colour of the shelves. The reading desks on the ground floor are tucked into the depths of the books with each desk supporting its own oil burning lamp and writing equipment.

I want to run around and look at everything, but I have to control myself. This *is* a library after all, and I have to respect the rules. I walk up the centre aisle, just trying to take it all in, before I turn my back to the bookcases and climb the set of stairs I'm closest to. The weight of my boots colliding with the metal stairs lets out a clang across the entire floor and I instantly want to shrivel up at the embarrassment of being so heavy footed. I wish I could be as nimble as Clydia sometimes.

I reach the top of the stairs and it opens to a whole other world. This is the only other floor, so I can see the high, *high*, ceilings. I lay across a section of large cushions and stare up. I can see parts of the sky through the stained-glass window that covers most of the roof. It domes above me and I'm annoyed that I didn't notice it from the front of the building. The sun shines in and colour fills the room. There are streaks of red, purple, yellow and blue, making the room look like a rainbow has been trapped inside.

I hear Addy and Flo clambering up the stairs, neither of them light footed either. The footsteps stop just before I hear 'blimey' slip out of Flo's mouth. I can safely say that I was *not* expecting architecture like this when we set out on this journey. So much time has been invested in making this place look magical. *Is Mary Wollstonecraft a witch too? Does Europe have witches?* I was always told that their witches are just women that act a bit weirdly.

They both settle down on the bed of grey cushions with me and we stay here in silence for a long time. Longer than I care to admit. The nerves about tomorrow are finally kicking in and I'm not sure if I'm ready anymore. I'm worried I'll trip up on my words, say the speech wrong or make us look like we're not competent. We're more than competent. I keep repeating the words *'I can do this; we can do this'* in my head. I have butterflies already.

The sun is getting higher in the sky and it's getting harder to keep my eyes open with it shining directly into them. 'We don't have long left until we need to make our way to Witchbank. Let's go and explore the other parts of the library.'

'I'm going to see if they have a physics section. I could use some more inspiration and information for future experiments.' *Of course Addy wants to learn now.*

'I'm going to find the fiction section. I could use a little light reading after all this madness.'

'I'll join you, Flo, I could use an escape, too.'

I browse the titles of some new romance fiction.

Even if I don't necessarily want my own love story, it's comforting to read about somebody else's. Flo comes up to me with two copies of the same book. *'Tales of a Teenage Witch'*.

'It seems really funny. Like a life we could have lived if these ridiculous laws weren't in place. It says on the back that the woman who wrote this book was arrested and taken to trial at Witchbank river. Royals attended the trial and everything because they thought she was a witch promoting the behaviour.'

'That sounds pretty cool, but also sad as heck. I'm definitely down to read it.'

'Perfect. Let's do it. As of tomorrow, we have a book club.'

We flick through the pages for a couple of moments, taking in the strangely comforting smell of parchment. My enjoyment isn't even disrupted by Flo's voice.

'What would our book be called? If there was one about our adventures?'

'Ours would be something truly dramatic. Something like *'Descendants of Despair'*.'

'I would give it something quirky, something kind. Something like *'Witches Aren't Wicked'*. We need people to know that our story isn't one of evil. It's born out of love, passion and hope. We're not all that bad once you get to know us.'

'I'd read it.'

'I don't think anyone else would.'

I roll my eyes and grab her hand. 'Let's go and find Addy before we're late meeting the others.'

I take one last look at the ceiling before starting my journey down the spiralling stairs. We find Addy towards the back of the library, with a stack of books on the reading desk that she's still piling up.

'Have you got enough there, kid?' I ask. She's in her own head and the sound of my voice jolts her out of it. Her body tenses as her head whips round from the shelf to face me, but she relaxes when she realises that it's just us.

'Oh heck, I thought you were someone I wouldn't want to see.' She glances over at the stack of books on the table and turns back to us. 'There are so many ideas that I could really use. I want to read all of them. There are so many women published here, too. I guess it helps that it is a library named after a woman.' Her voice is wild. I've never heard her so excited about, well, anything.

'You can bring as many as you can carry,' Flo says lightly. A touch of pride fills her words as she continues her sentence, 'and you can make as many notes as you want when this is over but for now, we've got to go and meet the others.'

She grabs the entire stack and I think she's going to fall over from the sudden weight. She sways for a moment but finally catches her balance before she can hit the floor and sprawl books everywhere. I grab a couple off the top and Flo follows suit.

'Thank you for your help. I'll be sure to include your names in my acknowledgements when I'm writing books like this. Well, it'll be a collection of research papers that form a book, but you'll be there.'

I hang my arm over her shoulders and guide her out.

Sometimes I think she's too young to be here.

Other times I remember that this girl is a blooming genius.

CHAPTER THIRTY-FOUR
June

'Hey!' I hear Clydia call from further down the river. 'How was the library.'

'It was beautiful. Really beautiful. You should definitely come with us next time.'

'Maybe we can all go?'

'Speaking of all, where the heck is Ottie? I know Addy and Flo are back down there a bit. Addy is struggling with some books. I assume Drusilla will be here in her own time too. That's five of us. I just don't see your new apprentice.'

'Ah, yeah, Ottie is up there.' She gestures to a tree just a few meters away. I look up and see a pair of legs dangling before I realise that Ottie is more than halfway up a tree.

'Ottilie Lambert, get down from there. What on Earth do you think you're doing?' I scream up at her. I hear her laugh hysterically before swinging her legs and dropping down to another branch. It's sturdy but I still wince at the thought of her falling. She cascades the tree like an acrobat. It's magical to watch but my heart is beating faster than it has done for a while.

'Why were you in a tree?'

'You get a perfect view of the entire grounds from up there.'

'Stay on the ground and we'll have a wander around. We don't need any more injuries on this journey.'

'Okay, okay. I can see Addy and Flo faffing over there. Are they okay?'

'Yeah. Should we go and meet them?' Clydia asks.

'You two head down to them,' Ottie says. 'I'll wait here for Dru. She shouldn't be long. I saw her coming through the entrance to the grounds with Laurence.'

'Laurence is with her? I wonder if he has good news about tomorrow,' I mention as we're walking to meet Addy and Flo.

'Well if he doesn't then we have the castle security pretty figured out,' Clydia reassures. I can't believe I forgot to ask about that.

'Oh yeah, how did that go? Is it complicated?'

'Not at all. The guards were barely awake. We can get in easy if they're like this tomorrow, too. Unless they have some kind of internal screening, but they seem trusting. I barely saw them bat an eye at anyone who entered.'

'Oh, that's great security. How haven't the

royals been murdered yet?'

'Everyone here seems to respect them.'

'I don't know why. The only remotely decent one is Laurence.'

We've only been walking for a minute or two when Ottie, Dru and Laurence come running up behind us. 'Hey guys, wait up.' It's the sing song tone in Drusilla's voice that catches my attention.

'Thanks for not being *too* late,' I joke.

'I'm always on time for important things.' She nudges me and I grin at her, grateful to see her happy.

'Let's get to the others. We have great news.' I've already guessed the great news, it's fairly obvious, but I'm so excited to hear it come out of her mouth that I start almost sprinting. I hear the others trail along behind me, shouting at me to slow down.

I'm elated.

I have so much energy.

This has been so much easier than we originally planned, and I'm suddenly way less nervous.

Laurence clears his throat when we're all together.

'I've managed to get you an audience for tomorrow morning. Arrive at the palace an hour after sunrise and I will come and meet you at the front gates. My father is allowing Thomas to sit in on his first audience as well as having me there. Please behave and don't emotionally scar this nine-year-old for life.'

'I make no promises,' Clydia jests but Laurence only glares at her. 'I'm kidding. My best behaviour. I promise.'

'You're the one I'm worried about most. Your best behaviour is mildly wounding someone rather than killing them.'

'My dagger and sword will stay firmly sheathed, but you'll be pleased to know that I won't be present in the audience. I'll be outside making sure nothing goes off plan from external sources.'

'Oh, please don't kill the guards either.' Laurence is starting to sound defeated already, and we haven't even told him the full plan.

'You really are no fun, Laurence Griffin. I hope you know that.'

'Don't you worry, Miss Tam, I already know.'

***

Laurence spends the next hour or so telling us the history of the Witchbank trials. They were horrible and it had all started because some children got sick. The local doctor diagnosed their symptoms as bewitchment by women who acted as nurses, nannies and even some less adjusted mothers. All because the children pointed out they had been in contact with them and they could have been the ones to bewitch them. These women were all tried in front of an audience and, quite obviously, found guilty. They were taken to Witchbank river, bound to a chair and thrown in. The chair was weighed down by rock, so they had sunk fast. If the witches survived the water trial, they would be hung. These events were a public affair so if any of these women really were witches, it was better to let the water take you. It was less embarrassing for yourself and for your family.

I watched my mother drown and I know I would fight if it happened to me. I would float. I would take my chance and I would speak out for all witches, young and old. I know they would gag me and bind my hands so I had no choice but to accept my fate, but I could find another way. There's always another way.

We're here to find another way.

As well as explaining what happened during the trials, Laurence tells us that later on there were sceptics who had conducted tests on the fungi that the children had consumed in the days leading up to their illness. It was discovered that this particular mushroom could induce vomiting, involuntary muscle spasms and hallucinations. The symptoms of the apparent 'bewitchings'.

'So, we will never know if those women really were witches or not, but either way they died in vein. They were wrongly convicted of a crime they didn't commit. Sometimes I like to sit here, next to the river, and think of them. I think of the lives they could have had with their children and how differently things could have ended if that doctor had just given the right diagnosis. It hits home with me in the same way I'm sure it does with each of you. Each of those children lost a woman who was important to them.'

'You have a way with words,' Dru says in awe. 'Do you think the same thing would happen now?'

The awe quickly turns to concern. 'Not legally, but I'm sure there are witch hunters out there who take the law into their own hands. They've heard the stories of the Witchbank trials, and they think drowning is the first step. During my rule, nothing like that will ever happen.'

'You have big dreams for your reign. I hope you get to enforce them all.'

'Me too.' He gives her a small smile.

Those two have a way of making every moment their own.

I'm happy for them, but I want to know more about the treatment of witches. Tomorrow is a big day and we need to be prepared for every scenario.

Every. Single. Scenario.

***

We're back at the inn, everyone completely exhausted from the long day. We ended up hanging around Witchbank river until the sun set and a new breeze gave the air a bitter chill. I hear my stomach growl and try not to pay attention to the army of faces that swing my way.

'Hungry, are we? I know a great little restaurant that you'll love. Follow me if you want to eat,' Laurence says.

It turns out that none of us had even eaten breakfast, so we all jump at the chance of some food.

The restaurant is on the same road as the inn, so we're there and eating in no time at all. Believe it or not, Laurence has pie with mashed potatoes which makes us all laugh. The rest of us have some kind of roast meat with mashed potatoes and mixed vegetables. I decide to try roast lamb for the first time and it's absolutely delicious. It's tender and juicy. I already know I'll miss food like this when we leave Fairpoint.

I eat slowly, savouring every bite of the meal. I'm almost finished when Clydia tells us that she has something to say.

'I have *never* told anyone this,' she starts, 'but you all need to know before tomorrow.' She takes a slow breath before continuing. 'If Prince Aeron is part of the audience tomorrow, he might recognise me. He's met 'Clyde' before. In unwelcoming circumstances. He saw my face and heard my voice. I'll stay as far away as I possibly can, but I just thought you all should know.'

'Sorry, what? Do you want to explain?' Addy asks.

'It's not a story for young ears, but you're mature, and I trust you with this information.' She looks at the youngest of us and smiles. A sad smile but a reassuring one, nonetheless. 'When I was back at the institute, I was called to do a job. A job for someone very important but they wouldn't disclose who. I watched my target for days. He didn't live close enough to a town for there to be any disturbances. It was just him. Alone and surrounded by fields.'

I look at the others. Everyone, including me, has confusion plastered right across their faces. Even Laurence who's glamoured. *Better to not be spotted by as many people,* he would say.

'I was watching him for a couple of days before I saw Prince Aeron come to the house…in the middle of the night. It was dark but I knew it was him from the way he held himself, tall, like there was no weight on his shoulders. He was wearing the royal dress suit, too so that helped. I won't tell you the details but basically I was sent to kill Aeron's lover, Damien, by I suspected, the king.'

'So *that's* where he used to sneak off to for days at a time,' Laurence realises aloud.

'I came back the next day, when Aeron wasn't supposed to be there, but I found the prince asleep in the bed so I assume he didn't leave the night

254

before, which makes sense if he used to disappear for days. I'm not proud of it and it is not something I did with an easy heart. Damien took his death like a champion. Maybe one day I'll tell you the full story, but that's all you need to know for now.'

We ask so many questions over dessert - rich dairy ice cream, delicious - all of which Clydia refuses to answer. I can tell that she doesn't feel comfortable talking about what she went through, but I want to know the full story either way. I take a back seat after most of my questions are shut down and let the others continue. I'll ask her in private after all of this is over.

'Leave her be,' Laurence says. 'She obviously doesn't want to talk about it right now. I'm going to go pay for all this and drag you lot back to the inn. You need to get a full night's sleep before tomorrow comes and you're not going to do that if I keep you out all night.'

He hurries us back and we separate into our rooms. I don't remember getting changed for bed or brushing my teeth. My eyes feel suddenly heavy and all I can think about is getting to sleep. This is a tiredness I have never experienced before. I feel like someone has dosed me a whole heap of valerian root mixed with a sprinkling of lavender just to calm the sudden reaction. Maybe they have. *What flavour ice cream did I get again?*

I don't remember my head hitting the pillow or

the sensation you get as you're slowly drifting off.

The next thing I know, Flo is shaking me awake and ushering me to get ready. The sun has risen, and we have less than an hour to be at the palace gates.

Today is the day.

Today is the day that we *will* be heard.

CHAPTER THIRTY-FIVE
Florence

'Florence, are you there?' I wake with a jolt that jumps me straight to a sitting position, but the room is still pitch black. It's the middle of the night and I could hear the gentle breathing of Drusilla and June next to me.

'Hello?' I whisper to the darkness. There's no response.

I lay my head back on the plush pillow and close my eyes. The room transitions from one darkness to another. I feel myself drifting back off to sleep when I hear the call of my name again. Something inside me knows what I have to do. I gently slide out of the bed and make my way to the bathroom. I close the door as silently as I can manage. So silently that the only noise made is the click of the lock.

'Hello?' No response. Again. I close my eyes even though there are no lights on. Submerging myself in the extra darkness. There's something about closing your eyes that makes the dark less scary because it is your own. It's impossible to see if this is going well, but I keep my eyes closed anyway. The words flow out of me like this is the only time I'm meant to say them. '*Visius spiritus.*'

Something brightens the room quickly before it simmers down to a gentle glow. The light is a stark contrast to what my eyes are used to. I open them slowly and there's a figure perched against the bath. It turns out that the glow is coming from a ball of light I didn't even realise that I created.

The figure is a woman. She's short, maybe the same height as Ottie, and her frame is small. Her features have been darkened in the low light. Her onyx hair seems to blend in with the darkness surrounding us. Her once rich brown eyes that complimented her umber skin are now almost as dark as her hair. She's a ghost of her former self but I guess that's what spirit sight is. I'm speaking to a ghost.

'Your Majesty,' I rasp, in shock that I've actually cast the spell correctly.

'Please, call me Cynthia.'

'Okay, Cynthia. Is there a reason you wanted to speak? How did you know how to contact me? How did I know how to contact you?'

'One question at a time, dear child.'

I gather my thoughts. 'How did you let me

know to contact you?'

'When somebody has a close connection to the next dimension from practicing the spirit sight, they are much easier to contact. Part of your soul becomes intertwined with what is referred to as 'the bridge'. The bridge between my dimension and yours. When you sleep, your mind is vulnerable to all sorts so I could get my message across to you. I just had to find where the part of your soul was held so I could merge it with some of mine.'

'So, our souls are merged?'

'The part of your soul that was taken by the bridge and a small part of mine, yes.'

'Why?'

'Because I have a message for you. A message from someone who has experienced the wrath of an angry king. Laurence called out to me, but he doesn't know I can hear him. He hasn't mastered the sight like you have. He told me about your plans for tomorrow. I came to tell you to be vigilant. You may think the king is on your side but there is always a hidden agenda with him. He won't hesitate to hurt you and claim your work as his own.'

'Laurence will be there. He's sworn to keep the king in a calmer temperament. I trust him.'

'You're right to trust Laurence but be cautious. He's a kind, caring soul but sometimes he can let his emotions cloud his judgement. I hoped it was something he would grow out of. Laurence behaves very differently around the king. He must prove himself or he won't be allowed the throne. Just be aware of everything happening around you. The king has a very short fuse.'

'Thank you, your Majesty. I appreciate the warning. I'll keep my guard up and my eyes peeled. My role is to be part of the demonstration, so I'll make sure that there are no backs to the king.'

'That would be wise. Do you have any other questions for me? I may not be able to pass through the bridge again for a while.'

'Just one. Should I tell Laurence about this?'

'No, not this time. I think we should let him believe that the sight isn't real for now. He will be able to reach me when he's ready.'

I nod. 'You're probably right.'

'I'm sorry to disturb you, young Florence. You have a big day coming up tomorrow. Go get some sleep. You only have a few hours before you need to be up.'

***

Surprisingly, Dru is the one waking me just before sunrise. She shakes me and asks if I want to use the toilet before she draws a bath. I turn back over before I can even reply. I'm assuming she took my silence as a no because I don't wake up again until she's just leaving the bathroom. I peer through the curtains. There's barely a sign of the sun which means I have enough time to draw a bath too.

Dru drops back onto the bed and closes her eyes, promising that she's not going back to sleep as I close the bathroom door.

The sun has almost fully risen by the time I emerge which means that we have less than an hour until we need to leave for the palace. I wake Dru up gently, but she soon jumps out of bed when she sees how bright the room is. Seeing her urgency makes me more frantic so I aggressively shake June awake. Her eyes shoot open and I usher her out of bed as quickly as I can. She'll have to clean her body quickly because we have to go sooner than we planned. We wanted to wake up before sunrise but that didn't happen, did it?

I dry my hair using 'siccum' and pull it back into a high ponytail. Better to get it out of the way now than get it cut or burnt off when the king finds out we're witches.

'I'm going to knock next door and see if they're ready. We need to leave in a few minutes.'

'Okay, Dru, be quick.' I tell her, like she doesn't already know.

She returns to the room a couple of minutes later with three girls in tow.

'Ready?' Ottie asks.

'We're good to go. Have you got the shield?' Addy turns and shows me it strapped to her back.

She looks like a superhero. 'Excellent.'

There's a shortcut near the inn where we could enter as women and exit as men with no suspicions raised. When we walk out the other side, we're just a few minutes away from the palace gates.

'Girls, I'm not feeling so great.' I think we all share the same nerves as Addy, but her and June have the most important parts, so I understand why she feels sick.

'It'll be over before you know it,' Dru says, 'and besides, we've got your shield to keep us safe.'

'If it works.'

'We know it does. You did a great job for such a small person. You'll be the smartest one in the room. Just remember that.'

'Thanks, Dru.'

Before I even have time to think about my nerves, we're at the palace gates. It's suddenly less beautiful and more terrifyingly massive when you have something important to do there. The adrenaline needs to kick in sooner rather than later or I'll be in a heap on the floor before the audience is out. The hour changes on the palace sundial just as Laurence appears at the gates. 'You're lucky. He's in a good mood today. The chef made his favourite pastries for breakfast.'

'He sounds like a very simple man to please.'

'He is, sometimes. Now let's go before he gets angry and accuses us of being late.'

I take the back of the line so I can look forward and make sure the rest of the girls are safe.

This could be the last time that we're all together. We could be killed on the spot as soon as the king finds out.

I just need this moment to take them all in.

I want to protect each one of them, but they can look after themselves and I know it better than anyone.

Honestly, I'm just proud of the women they're growing into.

CHAPTER THIRTY-SIX
Florence

I look at the doors to the audience chambers and have to steady myself against June. This is really happening. We have to impress the king without being killed. *Challenge accepted, I guess.*

Clydia and Ottie step to the side and let the five of us pass through the heavy doors. Each of us curtsying King Ernest as we enter. Laurence leads the way, followed by June, Drusilla, Adelaide and then me. The guards close the doors behind us, and I know that they'll be incapacitated within a couple of minutes. There'll be no disturbances and no response to the calls for help when we're exposed. It's our best chance of survival if I'm honest.

Laurence walks up the dais to take his seat next to King Ernest. I wasn't expecting to see Aeron here, but I guess it makes sense because he'll be the one using the shield. This is even worse than expected. An audience with the entire royal family. My stomach drops.

June is introducing us, and I take the time to re-adjust myself. I'm trying to keep a straight face, but I just want to laugh at how insane this situation is. I glance around the room trying to take it all in.

The royals definitely have a specific taste when it comes to interior design.

White marble covers the floor and shoots its way up to the ceiling in pillars. The thrones the royals sit on are gold with plush red cushions covering the seat and back. The same crimson red runs along the floor in a carpet leading up the dais and curtains drape across the windows to create shadows that break up the light.

I realise that I've been zoned out for a while and I force myself back to reality. I hear June speak the words 'which is why our inventor here, created this.' *It's almost my cue.*

'Your Royal Majesty, I ask you to consider this whilst you watch our demonstration. Would something with this much power benefit your forces? If just one shield can protect up to forty meters of space, depending on the wizard, imagine what a whole host of them could do. Imagine if every wizard in your force could hold one in battle.'

Joy radiates off Thomas's face, making his freckles scrunch into his small nose. His chocolate brown hair hangs in messy curls around his ears, which compliments his dark blue dress suit. The

blue of his robes is the same blue as his big eyes.
The colour and shape makes him look lost
compared to the rest of the family.

Laurence gives us all a reassuring smile. A nod
to go on.

I'm watching Thomas as June starts speaking
again and I wish he would stop biting the skin off
his lip. It's making them red and they'll be sore
tomorrow if he carries on. I turn to look at Aeron.
He doesn't look very impressed, but he hasn't seen
what it can do yet. I focus my attention back on the
King.

King Ernest is a larger man. He's tall but his
stomach is filled out to the point his trousers look
specially made. He's a solemn looking man, with
sloping brown eyes and a bald head that shines
enough to reflect light. He makes a lot of husky
grunts that I can tell are annoying June no end.

'I ask you to please remain silent during the
demonstration so you can admire the fine detail that
went into this project of defence.'

Oh gosh, it's time. I take a deep breath and step
forward. I don't feel ready but I have to be.

'My sisters' Adelaide,' she gestures to Addy
who drops her glamour, 'and Florence,' she then
gestures to me and I drop mine, 'will show you how
the shield works with various attacks.'

The royals go silent. All except Laurence who
stands up and starts to applaud. The king grabs his

arm and tries to pull him back down to his seat, but he remains standing.

Anger fills the king's eyes as he realises that he's been manipulated by a group of children. *Women*.

'Witches! Witches!' the king bellows. *Is he that scared of us?*

Obviously, there are no guards outside because Ottie and Clydia have taken care of them. They do, however, take the plan further and come into the room glamoured as the guards. Ottie turns to wink at me as she walks up the dais to stand next to Prince Aeron. He's so gob smacked that he doesn't see her remove the sword from next to his chair and replace it with a glamoured stick.

Clydia comes over to stand next to us, but she doesn't make to arrest us like the real guards would have done. Instead she takes the shield off Addy and asks me calmly to fire a spell at her.

I hesitate, not completely convinced that she knows what she's doing, but she gives me a single nod to let me know that it's going to be alright.

I take her word literally and throw a fire ball her way using *'ignis pila'*. She draws the shield to defend herself and uses the spell to extend the shield a short way. *'Virtus murum.'* There's a circle of refracted light around her. When the fire ball hits where the circle starts, it quickly spreads and fizzles out. There isn't even a hint of smoke. The fire just simply ceases to be.

She turns to the royal family and drops her glamour. The king turns visibly red and Aeron has no response. Laurence and Thomas on the other hand, stand up and cheer. Clapping away and completely blind to the growing rage from their father beside them.

'I do *not* understand. How did these *witches* get in here?' He turns to Laurence. I think steam is going to start coming out of his ears. 'You asked for this audience. Begged for it, in fact, but they are witches. This makes you a traitor to the throne and the law of the land. How do you want to explain *this*?'

Laurence turns white as a sheet as his sits back down silently. Apparently he's a lost little boy when it comes to being told off by his father. Thomas sees that Laurence is back in his seat and quickly decides to join him.

I realise now that we put our dreams in the hands of a boy. We thought he would help us persuade, he would help us fight. He would help us win. Nobody is on our side, though. Nobody is here to defend us.

Nothing has even gone to plan anyway.

We may as well have marched in here with no plan whatsoever.

It couldn't have gone any worse. This is the end. Everything we've worked for is gone.

We are going to die.

CHAPTER THIRTY-SEVEN
Drusilla

Clydia is crazy but I do what she asks. *The prince, that's a risky game to be playing.* I know she has her own plan now things have gone bottoms up, and we'll be informed on a need to know basis. There's screaming up on the dais between Aeron and Laurence. I'm so caught up in what's happening with Clydia that I don't hear anything of the argument until a word catches me off guard. It snaps me out of my thoughts.

Banished.

Did he say that Laurence is banished?

I'm sure the word banished just came from the king's tongue.

'You can't banish us!' Aeron screams at his father. 'I'm almost ready to take over the force. It'll take you ten years to train anyone else.'

'The only time you reacted was when you saw that one there,' he inclines his head to Clydia, 'and when you did react it wasn't anger. You weren't angry that *witches* have infiltrated the palace. You just tensed. There was no passion, no drive to get them away. A true commander would have jumped up and killed them all.'

'A true commander would lead his troops to victory. It doesn't matter I tensed. You were right. I tensed because I know about *her*. I know about your secret contract.'

Panic sets on the king's face. 'What do you mean?'

'Damien.'

I have to stop the fighting so I do it. I sling a spell at Thomas. He screams and Laurence lunges for him but Clydia activates the shield. The flames don't even have the chance get within two metres of them.

Thomas realises that he isn't dead and starts clapping. He's clearly amazed by what was happening in front of him and those big blue eyes got even wider. 'Again!'

'That's not a good idea, Tom. You might get hurt.'

'I'm nine now, Laurence. I know that I might get hurt and that's the fun of it.' His voice is full of sass.

'Well you *definitely* take after Aeron there.'

I raise eyebrows at Laurence in question. A

'*should I do it again?*' kind of look.

'You will not play these games anywhere near my son again.'

'Again!' Thomas calls.

Laurence gives me a challenging look.

I do it. I fling a fire ball at an innocent nine-year-old.

I do it over, and over, and over, until there's a scream.

I think for a second that I hit Thomas but he's still laughing.

The scream belonged to a girl.

Panic fills me.

I swing my head around. Everyone seems fine until...

June.

Red pools at my feet as I stand over her limp form on the floor. The king hasn't even given her the courtesy of taking his sword out of her skewered heart.

I drop to my knees.

I think a scream escapes me but I can't feel it.

My white cotton dress is filling with her blood.

Her eyes are open but they're glassy. All life had left them before she even hit the floor.

I want to close them but that means there's no going back.

I have to do it. She has to rest.

I want to lay down next to her and pretend that

271

I'm asleep.

Maybe I am asleep.

Flo hovers over me but the other girls keep their distance. I think it's more out of fear of getting too close to an obviously angry king rather than out of respect. She tries to lift me off the floor but anger is bubbling inside of me. I manage to drag myself upright, somehow. I apologise to June as I pull the sword out. I know she can't hear me but it feels right.

More blood spills free.

I turn to the king. Blade held high.

'Come here and fight me, you traitor. It's time to put Operation: Steel into practise.'

He laughs. The king of the Delgosi Isles just laughs in my face after murdering my best friend in cold blood. He's going to pay. We're going to fight and we're going to win.

'You don't want to fight me, witch. Plus, you have my sword so that wouldn't be a fair fight. How do I know that you and your little friends aren't manipulating me with magic either? This just isn't fair.'

'But it is fair to murder an innocent girl? It is fair to kill a woman for being a witch? Fighting me isn't fair but not letting women practice magic is? Nothing about your reign has been fair, Ernest, and now the tables have been turned.'

'How dare you address me like that? Have some

respect for your king.'

'I'll address you with respect when you earn it. Come here and fight me. If you win I'll be dead anyway, so it won't matter.'

He picks up the stick that Ottie glamoured as a sword when her and Clydia entered. She's now down with the others, sitting with June's body. I'm glad that she isn't alone.

He spins what he thinks is a sword in his hand to get the weight balanced. I know he can't hurt me, Ottie knows he can't hurt me and I'm pretty sure that June would have known that he can't hurt me. I'm not sure if the others know though.

He drags his large body down the dais and plants himself in front of me, his back to June and my friends, which means that I have to face them during this whole thing.

I don't know if it makes me want to fight more or if it's slowly bringing me down.

The king lunges for me and I quickly step out of the way. He's clearly lost his form over the years and doesn't quite know how to swing his own weight around anymore.

This could be over quickly but I don't want it to be. I want to cut him, hurt him, make him suffer.

I want to tear the monster apart.

I swing once, twice. Just like Laurence taught me. He isn't wearing any kind of body armour. I feign a left attack, which the king should have been able to easily block, before circling the blade around to attack the right. I nick him in the arm, right next the wrist. *The perfect shot to hinder somebody's fighting.* The sword will feel heavier for him now.

Clearly raging that I've already attacked, the king pounces.

Now, when I say pounces, I don't mean like a wild cat chasing its prey, agile and fierce. I mean like a domestic cat that's trying to bat food out of their owner's hand; lazy but entitled.

The king starts his attacks but never gets to finish them because I easily jump out of the way at the last minute. He's slow with a sword. Slower than me, and I've only just learnt how to fight with one.

I don't see Laurence move from his chair. I don't see him approach the girls and ask for Clydia's dagger. I don't see him until one hand appears in front of his father's throat and the other around his body, pulling him back. By then, it's too late.

'This has gone on long enough!' he shouts, whilst drawing an almost perfectly straight line with the blade.

Blood sprays from the wound and covers me even more.

I'm suddenly repulsed at the state of me.

The king's eyes widen with the realisation of what's happened. Laurence is holding the king upright and I watch his head loll forward as the life drains out of him.

He checks the pulse at the king's wrist.

'Nothing.'

Remorse shows on his face as he drops the king's body to the floor and falls backwards.

I would have thought Thomas would be screaming at the scene, but he and Ottie are nowhere to be seen. I'm glad she got him out before he could see anything worse. This isn't how Laurence wanted Thomas's first audience to go. He'll be scarred after seeing the events of today.

'Looks like you've finally got your own way, little brother.' I hear Aeron say from behind me. His voice is harsh but I can detect some admiration, some pride. 'You can finally start your rule. Create the life that you so dream of.'

Laurence looks at him, face turning from white to green. He strides over to Aeron who grabs his shoulders to hold him up. Laurence quickly spins away from him and vomits all over the floor. 'Wha... wha...what have I done?'

'You've done what we've all wanted to do for a while.' He ropes his arm around Laurence's shoulders again and squeezes the sides of their bodies together. 'Congratulations. You've made your first big decision as the ruler of the Delgosi Isles.'

Laurence seems to be in shock and I want to run to him more than anything, but I need to check on

June. I need to make sure that she's okay. Well not okay but, you know, I need to be there with her.

I want to drop to the floor and crawl to her, but instead I walk on shaky legs to the group of girls surrounding a puddle of red. Only then do I kneel down and stroke her hair, a cloud of chestnut brown that's now matted with splatters of dry blood.

I look around the room at the bloodshed and the bodies.

The puddles of blood match the crimson of the carpet.

This room was expecting death, and death is what it got.

CHAPTER THIRTY-EIGHT
Clydia

I try to pull Dru away from June's body, but she isn't having it. I thought for a second that she was going to try and shake her awake, but she doesn't. She just sits with tears streaming from her eyes whilst stroking the hair away from her face.

We're all crying, but Dru is definitely taking this the worst. Her and Flo have already lost someone dear to them on this journey so I'm positive this hits even harder. I've seen death more times than I can count but the death of someone you really care about, someone you really love, will always shock you to your core.

Laurence snaps out of his shock when he sees Dru kneeling in a puddle of red. Her eyes are raw from the tears that have been falling for some time. His legs really don't look like they can support him, but he makes his way over here anyway. He drops down next to her and I watch her posture change. She slumps over more, her body tenses and her eyes close. It's like she knows he'll force her away.

'I'm sorry,' the words are barely a whisper on his lips. She doesn't respond. If anything, she sobs harder. He looks to Flo for advice, but she simply shrugs. We're all just trying to process the scene in front of us.

'Try and get her out of here. Get her somewhere safe where she can clean up,' I say to him. He nods like he's never experienced the motion before and drags himself up. His legs seem much surer of themselves now. He bends back down, but not into a kneel, instead he places his arms underneath Dru's and pulls her to a standing position. Laurence throws her arm around his neck whilst holding her waist with his left hand. He tucks his right hand underneath her knees and lifts her body up. He pulls Drusilla into him as he takes one last look around the room before disappearing through the same doors we came through.

'I'm going to go and find a doctor,' Flo announces. I can tell that she doesn't want to leave June either, but someone has to arrange for both her and the king to be taken away from here. 'Aeron, could you join me? You obviously know your way around and I could use a hand if I'm completely honest.' She looks at him with heavy eyes, but he doesn't reply. Instead, he just walks towards Flo and takes her hand.

'Can you walk or should I carry you out like my brother did with your friend?'

I watch her draw back her hand and swing it at his face.

She slapped him. Florence Flynn just slapped a prince of the Delgosi Isles.

He grabs her wrist but she whips it free from his grasp.

'Don't speak of someone in mourning like that. Especially not my sister.' I think she's going to hit him again, and I'm cheering for her because of it, but she just rips her hand from his and strides out of the room. At least the sadness has turned to anger so she can get this done quickly. Aeron follows her out but hangs back a meter or so. *Smart*. Flo can switch again at any minute and after the sound that first slap made, I wouldn't want to be in the firing zone either.

Addy shuffles over to me and places her head in my lap.

'I can't look at her anymore,' she sobs. 'I keep thinking that she's going to wake up because she just looks like she is sleeping but she's not. I'm not going to be able to tell her any of the things from the books. I'm not going to hear her voice. I'm going to miss her singing whilst she cooks.'

'I know, kid, I'm going to miss her too. We used

to stay up until way past midnight talking about what we both wanted in the future. She wanted to take you to Europe, you know. She wanted you to see all the science stuff out there. She wanted you to be inspired, to be the Marie Curie of the Delgosi Isles.'

Addy squeezes her eyes shut and she weeps into me. I stroke her hair the same way Dru was stroking June's. It's comforting. I can see why she did it. I don't know how long I've been sitting here stroking Addy's hair but at some point, her sobs give way to heavy breaths. She has managed to cry herself to sleep.

I make a vow to myself, a whisper into her soft blonde hair, to always protect her.

I'm numb by the time Flo and Aeron return with a doctor trailing behind them. The doctor gasps as he surveys the room. He has one of those faces that can easily blend into a crowd. There's nothing distinguishable about him other than the medic bag he carries.

'What happened here?'

'There was a conflict of interest,' Aeron replies.

'Treason?'

'I think the new king would disagree.'

The doctor takes a clipboard and a pot of ink from his bag. He keeps his quill in a separate box in his pocket. I don't know what he's writing. They're clearly dead. He works in silence until he presents

Aeron with two certificates of death. 'Take care of these until Prince Laurence can receive them. I'll ask my assistants to come and collect the bodies. You might want to ask your most trusted member of the staff to get the floor cleaned, too. There can be no evidence of what happened here today, or the kingdom will reject Laurence's claim.'

'I'll clean the floor up,' I offer. 'Just get me the things I need to do it.'

'I'll help. We can take both June and the king somewhere together too. Just let me know where and make sure the hallways are clear. Nobody else needs to know what happened here,' Flo adds.

Aeron leaves with the doctor and returns a few minutes later with some rags, a mop and water. He also has a couple of large red sheets hanging over his arm.

'The hallways are clear, just head straight when you come out of here. The first set of stairs you come to will be on the right. Head down them and you'll find an empty room other than two low beds. Leave them there.' He throws the sheets at us. 'Cover them with these too, just in case of prying eyes.'

'Why are you helping us? I thought you were... I don't know... evil.' I roll my eyes at Flo's outrageous question.

He just winks at her. A wink that can be interpreted a thousand ways.

'I need to go and thank my brother for what he did today.' Aeron makes to leave but I stop him.

'Take her with you. Find somewhere to keep her safe. Let her sleep as long as she needs and don't make any jokes about carrying her. She's just a child.' She gestures to Addy still in my lap.

'A child that you decided to bring along.'

'That *child* invented *that* shield.' I point to it on the floor. It looks ironic, just lying in the middle of a room with a dead body on either side.

'Yeah, I actually need to speak to her about that.'

***

We're all gathered around a table in what I assume is a banquet hall. There's so much food piled in front of us, but Aeron is the only one eating. *How does he not care?* I'm pushing a perfectly crisp chunk of potato around my plate when he pipes up.

'About this shield,' he looks to Addy. 'How do we make more?'

'I can make them for you?' she offers, nothing but fact in her tone.

'The guys of the force will reject it if they know it's made by a girl. Let alone a *witch*.'

She looks hurt at what he thinks is a flippant comment.

'If you want the shield, brother, you give her credit. You let her show the 'guys' how it works, and you will not jest her in front of them. Do you understand me?'

I've known Laurence just a few days but I can already tell that he is not a force to be reckoned with.

Aeron doesn't respond to Laurence, in fact, he continues to speak to Addy. 'What do you say, witch? I'm sure my brother will make sure that you can't be arrested or killed for using your powers anyway. If I'm honest with you, we kind of need something like this.'

Her voice is small compared to his, but equally as mighty. 'Sure.'

'He's right,' Laurence says after a few minutes of awkward silence. 'As soon as the funeral is over and the coronation is complete, you will all be able to live in peace.'

He looks at each of us individually. 'In fact, I would like you to all stay here. We could use the strengths of each and every one of you.'

Nobody moves. Nobody speaks.

I'd dragged the body of my best friend around the halls of this palace and now we're sitting having dinner like it wasn't just a few hours ago.

He's unbelievable.

A big part of me wants to stay though.

I excuse myself from the table and the rest of the girls follow, leaving the future king of the Delgosi Isles and his brother, the commander of their troops, alone.

***

Laurence has provided each of us with our own room in the guest wing, but we all end up piled in Flo's bed. A bed big enough to fit five is another luxury that none of us have ever experienced. We've seen a lot of luxuries recently and I'm very thankful for them. It doesn't make processing today any easier though.

'This feels wrong,' Dru says from next to me. I squeeze her tight. Flo and I are on the outside, Ottie and Dru are next to us and Addy is slap bang in the middle. Two lines of defence to keep her safe.

'Doesn't it? If it were anyone else, she would be here giving us a big speech about how they *wouldn't* want us to mope around. About how we got what we wanted in the end. About how we all came into this knowing it was dangerous and there could be sacrifices.' I feel like part of her is channelling through my words.

'At least we will always have these,' Ottie says, holding her wrist in the air. *The bracelets*. I had completely forgotten about them. I'm so used to it being on my wrist. I twirl it around and around, reminding myself of its presence. I've never been a person to wear jewellery and have nice things, but this is special. This will stay on my wrist until the day I die.

'The Queen warned me about this.' I pull myself up so my head is resting on my hand before staring at Flo. I raise my eyebrows in shock and she continues. 'Last night, she told me to keep an eye on the king because he would strike when we weren't expecting it. She told me to make sure nobody turned their back to him, but I was so caught up in what was happening that I let my guard drop. This is my fault.'

What?

'This isn't your fault. This is King Ernest's fault for being ignorant and aggressive.'

'The Queen told me.'

'The Queen is dead. You know she is.'

'I spoke to her. She called to me through the sight.'

I drop myself back down onto the pillow and stare up at the ceiling. 'You used the sight?'

'Yeah.'

'Do you think you can do it again?'

'I'm not sure. The Queen came to me in my sleep and guided me to her.'

'Can we try?'

We climb out of bed as Flo tells us to turn off the lights and stay silent. We shift around until we're sat in a circle on the hard floor. A small ball of warm light appears in her hand and casts a dim light over our faces.

'Just so you know this may not work. Please don't get your hopes up too much.'

'We're all here for you,' I say, 'and you're going to do great. You're a strong witch, Flo.'

'Okay.' She takes a deep breath and shifts her hands. '*Visius spiritus.*'

Nothing happens.

She forces her eyes shut and tries again. '*Visius spiritus.*'

It's like she goes to another place. Almost like she lets part of herself go. Her light grows quickly before cutting out. She sparks it up again and suddenly we're circling the Queen of the Delgosi Isles.

I thought only Flo would be able to see her, but here she is, right in front of my eyes.

'Cynthia,' she says, relief filling her voice. 'We lost one of our own today. May we speak with her?'

The Queen smiles sadly. 'She will not be able to reach you until she has had an official send off. I can tell her how to reach you as soon as her physical body is laid to rest.'

'We haven't planned a funeral yet.' The mood in the room shifts from surprise to sadness again.

'I'm sorry, Florence. I wish I could help you.'

'It's okay. I can try and find her once her body is at rest.'

'I will help you find her when that day comes but for now, I can tell you that she is safe here. Her spirit has passed over the bridge.'

The mood shifts again. Another air of relief crosses the room.

'Thank you for letting us know that she is safe, your Majesty. Laurence is devastated about what he did to his father. It was an impulse.'

'He did what he thought was right. The sign of a true king. I'm proud of him for making a big decision, and between you and me, I'm excited to be with Ernest again.' She winks at Flo and steps out of the circle so she can look at all five of us. 'She doesn't blame any of you for what happened today. She told me that you won and it was worth the sacrifice.' There's a chorus of sobs as we all start to cry. Flo more than any of us. She can no longer blame herself.

She must have lost concentration because the light shuts out.

She screams and tries to spark it again, but the Queen is gone.

It's okay, though, because June's spirit is safe.

Our friend, our sister, is in the safe hands of Cynthia Griffin. The true Queen of the Delgosi Isles.

CHAPTER THIRTY-NINE
Florence

'Is everyone ready?' I look at each of my sisters. We've become much closer over the past few days here at the palace. Something I didn't think was possible. Laurence has been so generous, too. He had his best seamstress make each of us a mourning dress. It's custom to wear black to a funeral so that's what we've got. I watch as Clydia straps her knife to her ankle and covers it with her boot. She has to protect us all, even if she *is* in mourning.

Today isn't just the funerals, though, it's Laurence's coronation, too. June's funeral was going to be just us, but Laurence insisted that he would like to bring Charles and Aeron to pay their respects. I don't mind at all, and to be perfectly candid, June loved attention. The more people that are there, the happier she'll be.

The palace is still in mourning too, but everyone is rushing around to prepare for the king's funeral so they don't notice us move through the corridors. The king's service is being held in the chapel, but June loved to be outside, so Laurence has arranged to bring her to the gardens. We arrive at the entrance to the gardens where Charles meets us. He leads us through the winding paths until we reach a collection of viburnum plants where Laurence is waiting with Aeron. *How did he know? Had she told him?*

There had been nobody to clean up her body, so the casket is closed and placed on a delicate iron table. Small pieces of wood have been woven together to make her casket look like a picnic basket. The entire thing looks perfectly June.

I place my hand on it and the other girls follow.

'I laid her in there myself,' Laurence says, his voice gentle. 'She's comfortable. She looks peaceful.'

There are so many things that I want to say but no words come. Instead, we all stand there sobbing over the case that is housing our sister's body.

I finally get myself together and clear my throat. 'June cared about everyone around her. She cared about us more than she cared about herself. She always said exactly what you wanted to hear, even if you didn't know it yourself. Her life has been ended much too young, but I know she would rather it end for something worthwhile. I'll never forget her kind heart, so this isn't goodbye. She'll always be with me. She'll always be with each and every one of us.'

I can tell that Clydia is trying to get some kind of speech out, but she's too choked up. She closes her eyes in preparation and I place my spare hand on her back, just between her shoulder blades.

'Thank you for making our tiny little house a home,' she starts. 'Thank you for making it easier to come home every night knowing that tomorrow was going to be an even better day. You were my sunshine on a rainy day. I will always hold you in my heart and in my soul, June bug.'

Somebody wheezes but nobody else speaks.

We've decided not to bury her body, but to turn it to ash and take it back to Eastfall. We want to spread her ashes around the viburnum patch that will now be fully in bloom.

We take our hands off the casket, but Drusilla has chosen to complete the final ritual. Her prayer is broken with sobs, but the goddess would understand.

'Goddess, I ask of you. Please untie the knots. Her soul belongs to you, her body belongs to us and her spirit belongs to the next life. She can no longer be held as one. I ask you to keep her safe. I ask you to keep us strong. I ask you to let her soul live on. Amen, and so long.'

She forms the spell with her hands, but the words are barely a whisper. *'Intus uri.'*

We step back as the flames lick the casket and

our sister's body turns to ash. The smell is awful but we all stand strong.

The flames die down and the tears slow.

All that's left of our sister is a few ashes on a cast iron table.

'She would have liked it here,' Clydia says lightly. 'Do you think that maybe we can let her live on in these gardens? Spread her over the flowers that bloom in different seasons.'

I start to cry again but Addy leans in and hugs me. If she can be strong then so can I. 'I think that's a great idea. She was always one for an adventure.'

'We'll leave the five of you alone,' Aeron announces. 'Our father's funeral will be starting soon and we need to welcome guests. Please don't feel obliged to attend. I know he is the reason we are out here, and as heartless as people think I am, I understand how hard it is to say goodbye to someone you love.'

He looks directly at Clydia as she's wiping her nose. 'You took Damien from me, but I would never wish that pain upon anyone. I'm truly sorry for your loss.'

With that, Aeron turns on his heel and leaves. Charles follows him right away, but Laurence stays long enough to give Drusilla a quick kiss on the head and a promise that he will find her this evening.

I gently collect June's ashes into a vase.

Addy sprinkles some over the viburnum.

Ottie sprinkles some over where the daffodils will bloom in the spring.

Drusilla sprinkles some over where the sunflowers will bloom in the summer.

Clydia darts for a chestnut tree towards the back of the gardens. The conkers will fall in the autumn which, I guess, means it will in bloom. She sprinkles the last of the ashes there and draws her knife.

'What are you doing?' I ask.

'You'll see.'

She takes the blade to the bark of the tree and starts scraping. When she's finished, June's initials are staring back at us.

JD.

June Dodgson.

'Now she will always be part of this palace. Until they chop the tree down that is, but if we tell Laurence it won't be until we're all dead anyway."

'It's perfect.'

I stand and stare for a moment. It really is perfect.

I blink back my tears and turn to my remaining sisters. 'Let's leave her to rest. We have a coronation to attend.'

CHAPTER FORTY
Florence

The sun is starting to set by the time everyone has their dresses on, and the coronation starts at dusk. We haven't left each other all day so getting ready takes much longer than expected.

'Zip me up?' Dru asks. Her velvet dress is an emerald green that makes her red hair stand out. The dress exaggerates her figure in all the places I envy. It's tight to her body but pools at the floor. I've never seen her look as beautiful as she does right now.

My dress is crimson red. It's made of silk and ties up around my neck. It's tight around the top half of my body before water-falling down from my waist. My hair up in an intricate bun so you can see the bow that forms at the back of my neck.

Clydia's dress is dove grey. She insisted on it being tight around her slim frame before puffing out at the bottom so she can still carry her knife around her ankle. The bottom has diamonds winding up to her knees and it makes the dress seem like it moves with magic. The seamstress says this was what they call a mermaid dress. 'I've never been more uncomfortable in my life,' she moans as I'm zipping up the back.

Ottie's plum dress is a similar cut to mine, but rather than falling to the floor, it ends at her knees. She has diamonds forming the heels of her shoes that she wants to show off and I really don't blame her. She's helping Addy lace up the back of her dress when I ask if they're nearly ready to leave.

'One minute,' she replies. Addy's dress makes her look like a princess. It's a champagne pink and the bottom is covered in glitter. The sleeves cap off at her elbow so the bottom of dress puffs out from where they end. The glitter sparkles as she spins in the light of the setting sun. 'Ready.'

'Well, ladies. Let's go and watch our prince become a king.'

***

The staff have obviously spent more time with the funeral arrangements because the decoration in here is simple. A white carpet runs from the doors to the dais and there are flowers scattered around the room. I look up to take in the high ceilings and string lights are hanging overhead. It looks more like a small wedding than a coronation, but everyone will be too upset to care, I suppose. People are piling in the room after us and Aeron gestures the five of us to the front row. 'By Laurence's request,' he says. We take our seats and a few minutes later someone starts playing an organ. The song is soft as Laurence is led down the centre aisle by a team of guards. When he reaches the front, the officiant asks him to kneel as the guards disperse.

'Prince Laurence, future King of the Delgosi Isles, do you wish to accept this crown and all of the responsibility that comes with it?'

'I accept.'

'Do you swear to protect your kingdom for as long as you live?'

'I swear.'

'Do you promise to rule with your own best judgement?'

'I promise.'

'Then please rise and face your subjects.'

Laurence is wearing a royal blue cloak that covers his black mourning outfit. I glance at Thomas and Aeron, both of whom are wearing outfits that match the colour of his cloak. He turns to face the room with his head held high.

'I place this crown on your head, and this sceptre in your hand, as a symbol of your rule. Long live the King.'

'Long live the King,' the room chants back.

'As my first act of King, I would like to make you all aware that witchcraft is no longer outlawed. Any witches in this room, and all over the Delgosi Isles, may practice as they please.' He gestures to us and I shuffle down in my seat. 'These five women fought for something they believe in and I urge you all to take the chance to speak to them this evening. Listen to their stories and take some of their courage away with you. This will be a new age and I hope that you all stand with me.'

Drusilla beams at him and he gives her a huge smile back before taking a seat on the throne that sat on top of the dais. We all rise and pledge our allegiance to the new king.

The chairs are cleared out and music starts to play. Laurence hands his sceptre to Charles and starts down the steps. He takes Dru's hand and sweeps her away into the crowd.

'Well, I guess we won't see her for the rest of the evening,' Clydia jokes.

'Honestly, I'm just here for the food,' Ottie replies. There's a table to the side of the room filled with finger food and the four of us make a beeline there. We may look the part, but we definitely don't fit in here.

***

Long after we've eaten ourselves stupid, I grab

Clydia's hand and drag her to the middle of the room. She, in turn, takes Addy's hand who then reaches Ottie's. It's a chain reaction.

'I hate dancing,' Clydia complains but I act like I can't hear her.

'Oh, stop complaining,' comes a voice from behind us. Dru jumps in the middle and starts moving her body in ways I can only dream of doing.

'I guess King Laurence has officially declared himself as unavailable after dancing with you,' I say to her.

'It looks like it,' she replies. 'But as good of a dancer as he is, I would much rather be here showing you lot up.'

'Of course you would.'

We dance until our feet are sore and we're belly laughing at how awful we are.

People look disgusted with us, but they don't know what we've been through.

It feels good to feel free.

We are.

We are finally free.

EPILOGUE
Florence

It's been a month or so since June passed but we decided to stick around a while. It turns out, we actually enjoy living in a palace full of opportunities. Let me fill you in on what everyone is doing now.

Aeron accepted Addy's help and she's showing him how to work the shield to its full potential. She's also using the books she got from the library to develop it further, but I don't really understand how. It doesn't make much sense to me.

When Laurence found out that Ottie made an excellent challenge in taverns, he asked her to be his spy. Spend time around the city, listening out for anything people are saying. See if anyone suspects anything, that sort of thing. It also wouldn't be the end of the world if she beat a few of his advisors at card games either.

Clydia is working with the King's guard. She

told us about Laurence asking her to stick around and act as his bodyguard. We all laughed because it makes complete sense. They argue like it's nobody's business and I'm sure Charles has a few words to say about her, but it's a great partnership and Laurence says he always feels safe with her around.

Laurence is now officially courting Dru, so she's been spending a lot of her time with his advisors learning about how it all works. She's been asked to keep the details to herself, but she shares some stuff with us. I wish I could tell you more, but I'm sworn to secrecy. They keep calling her Madame Drusilla which she mocks in their fancy voices when we're in private. They seem happy together, and we're all happy for them.

And me? I think I have the best job. Over the first week or so of us being here I was thinking about training as a doctor. I didn't know what I wanted to do but Laurence said that Thomas had been asking about me a lot, so I now look after him when he's not in lessons, and he's a really fun kid to hang out with. He has an incredible imagination and he loves to play pranks, too. I ask Dru for more ideas most nights. After everything this poor kid has been through, his smile never falters. It's contagious.

I spend my days smiling with him, whilst the others do what makes them happiest.

We're free to do what we love because a new

reign has begun.
An honourable and *equal* reign.

Acknowledgements

I wish I could just write a list of names of the people I would like to thank, but that's not really how these things go, so I guess it's time to get sentimental.

To Mum, you've spent 24 years of your life guiding me in the right direction and I'm grateful for that every single day. I would never have been the bookworm I am today without you pushing books into my lap. Your kindness, thoughtfulness and generosity are all traits I am grateful to have received from you. I love you to the moon and back.

To Matt, thanks for always keeping me grounded. You're a bit of a tool but you're a good enough lad to get a little line or two in my book.

To Leigh, cheers poohead.

To Jord, you're alright.

To my sisters, my triplets, my everything. Amy and Emily. Thank you for your unconditional support and love. You always keep me going when I get knocked down. Also, thank you to my Auntie Deb and Uncle Steve, for acting like a second set of parents.

To my lady and my other lady, thanks for loving me and

supporting me even though you never have any idea what I'm talking about. You make my heart full.

To Tonicha, without you, I never would have made it through our English A-Levels. Thanks for always skipping sixth to go to McDonalds with me.

To my bars, Alice and Ellie. 15 years. 15 whole years of being best friends. Thank you for always having my back and for putting up with all of my wild ideas. Thank you for always reading my awful first drafts just because you're excited for the story and thank you for putting up with my constant breakdowns. My life would be empty without you both.

To Lauren, my go to girl, my number 1 cheerleader and my emotional support group. I'm so proud of you and everything you've achieved. Thank you for all of the adventures that we pass off as writer's retreats and brainstorming sessions on video chat. This book would be nothing without you, Prince Laurence. Oh, and also, thank you for Tony.

To Chloe, I wanted to write your acknowledgement in Korean, but it would have just been a whole mess of Google translate symbols. Addy would be proud of the amazing woman she's modelled after. We may speak once every 16,000 years because we both suck at replying to texts, but you're still my soul sister, my witch in training, my one true love. Thank you for encouraging me to write whatever my heart desires.

To my pests, Char and Colin. Thank you for being part of the *iconic trio that plagued our workplace. Your unconditional support and kindness kept me going through the months of editing and writing this thing.*

To Beck and Lou, thank you for welcoming me into this little SRL family. You're my dream colleagues as well as my dream friends. I've never met a pair of people I just click with so easily. I am so so SO proud of you and your awesome books.

To Rosie, thank you for bringing my gorgeous cover into the world. I wouldn't trust anyone else with it and I'll be forever grateful that you accepted the challenge.

Finally, thanks to SRL Publishing. I've never experienced a company so determined yet relaxed. Thank you for letting me have some input over the entire process and trusting me to actually do a good job. Thank you for picking up this tiny little book that's meant to empower the next generation. I hope we get to bring freedom and fun to a whole load of young minds.

There's so many more of you that I would like to thank, but I think I've rambled on enough. Just know that if you've had an impact on my life, you've probably influenced part of this book. You'll just have to imagine that there's enough space on these pages for me to include you.

That's it. That's the end.